More praise for *Down by the Riverside*

"This is a distinguished debut. The distinctive setting and eccentric cast of characters who call Shady Grove home are the set-up for a great series."   —*Publishers Weekly*

"Love, death, healing, redemption, and the deep connections that can grow between strangers are at the heart of this gentle mystery."   —*The Pilot*

"*Down by the Riverside* is a lyrical mystery that rolls along much like the great Mississippi River it portrays. Sometimes gentle, sometimes fierce, always the currents below the surface hide far more than they reveal. With beautifully crafted prose, Jackie Lynn weaves a tale of outcasts living along a riverbank, who while seeking the truth about a drowning, ultimately find both love and redemption."

—Sallie Bissell, author of *In the Forest of Harm*

"A delightful whodunit . . . Lynn provides a deep Mississippi mystery starring a likable woman who starts to obtain a sense of achievement, redemption, and worth."   —Harriet Klausner

"Jackie Lynn's lyrical prose creates a richly diverse cast of characters brought by fate or chance to the Shady Grove Camp-ground on the banks of the timeless Mississippi River. Lynn's writing touches the everyday with a golden glow, turning the simplest moments into profound truths."

—Vicki Lane, author of *Signs in the Blood*

DOWN
BY THE
RIVERSIDE

A Shady Grove Mystery

JACKIE LYNN

ST. MARTIN'S MINOTAUR
NEW YORK

www.minotaurbooks.com

Library of Congress Cataloging-in-Publication Data

Lynn, Jackie.
   Down by the riverside : a Shady Grove mystery / Jackie Lynn.
      p.   cm.
   ISBN-13: 978-0-312-37127-2
   ISBN-10: 0-312-37127-6
   1. Camp sites, facilities, etc.—Fiction. 2. North Carolina—Fiction. I. Title.

PS3612.Y547 D69 2006
813'.6—dc22

                                                                    2005033985

First St. Martin's Minotaur Paperback Edition: June 2007

10 9 8 7 6 5 4 3 2 1

IN LOVING MEMORY OF
LARRY MAURICE FRANKS
JULY 19, 1942—JUNE 12, 2004

AND HE SHALL BE LIKE A TREE
PLANTED BY THE STREAMS OF WATER

ACKNOWLEDGMENTS

The author gratefully acknowledges Linda McFall for believing in this series and for helping move the story along; Sabrina Soares Roberts for her very keen eye; Sally McMillan for her support and grace; and the staff at Tom Sawyer's Campground in West Memphis, Arkansas, for creating a lovely place where stories can happen.

I Love all Things which Flow

—attributed to Edward Abbey

Gonna lay down my burden

Down by the riverside

Down by the riverside

Down by the riverside.

Gonna lay down my burden

Down by the riverside

Gonna study war no more.

THE
FIRST
DAY

Trouble don't come always
That's what the preachers say
But I've seen so much trouble
I'm weary every day.

I think I'll sail to kinder ports
I think I may be free
I think maybe today's the day
Love's gonna come to me.

ONE

Three days before I arrived in West Memphis, Arkansas, just before dawn, it was said that Lawrence Franklin V, the undertaker from the south side of town, dressed in his finest black suit, cut a small sprig of a purple flower—lilac from his mother's garden—placed it in the narrow slit sewed in the corner of his lapel, got into his car, drove down to the Mississippi River, walked past her muddy banks, and drowned.

He was fifty-six years old, a confirmed bachelor, the son of Lawrence Franklin IV, grandson of Lawrence Franklin III, great-grandson of Lawrence Franklin, Jr., great great-grandson of Lawrence Franklin, Sr. Across generations and at consecutive intervals, each one of the Franklin men had served as the director and owner of Franklin's Family Funerals.

They had buried slaves, former slaves, children and grandchildren of slaves, and many more who had lived their lives in freedom. Like most of us, Lawrence Franklin V bore out his fifty-six years somewhere between the two states of human existence. He was never somebody else's chattel, but more often than not, his dreams and memories were bound by old and indelible chains.

Of course, at the time of my arrival I knew nothing of a dead man bearing the same last name as my mother, the same name I would claim for myself. I knew nothing of Lawrence Franklin V or of the watery details of his suicide. I knew nothing at all of life and death in West Memphis, Arkansas. I was a woman swimming through my own muddy currents, trying to keep from drowning in my own undertakings. I had no knowledge of a funeral director whose lungs filled with river water and whose heart had just been satisfied.

I was not planning to stay in West Memphis. I was on my way southwest, to New Mexico or Arizona, to work as a traveling nurse or maybe even something completely out of my profession like a museum director or a manicurist. I was on my way to somewhere far and fast from Rocky Mount, North Carolina. I was on my way to anything other than life familiar.

Arkansas was supposed to be only a gas stop. Maybe time enough for lunch or a good walk. I was not expecting to stay. But my 1987 Ford Bronco, pulling my travel trailer, sputtered and skipped down the interstate, finally stalling at the Chevron station at Exit 280, just across the Memphis Bridge.

It was a man by the name of Ledford Pickering who told me about the Shady Grove Campground, down past the oil rigs and the horse pastures, across the railroad tracks and out into the tree-lined path that opened out on the river like the dreams of some boat captain.

He told me about the campground after he heard the station manager say he couldn't get to my problem until later in the afternoon, that he wasn't sure the Bronco would be fixed by morning. Ledford Pickering was standing close enough to weigh out the details of my situation and was interested enough to think of some solution.

Ledford, a career trucker who had just finished his shift and had driven his old Ford pickup over to the station to fill up before heading out for a few hours of late-day fishing, offered to hook my camper up to the back of his truck and take me to the site. He was set up to pull his boat and trailer, but since he had brought only his truck to the station and since he lived near the campground, he didn't think there was any problem driving me over.

The mechanic at the station winked at Ledford like he had seen this before, smiled, and turned his head aside so as not to watch me as I made up my mind. And even though my mama was sure to sit up in her grave making a face wide with shame and Rip would have never believed I would do such a thing, I jumped in the truck with a man I didn't know, hooked my camper up to his trailer hitch, and let him take me to a campground that may or may not have existed. I was at a time and place in my life where I was ripe for adventure.

It was just after the intersection with Highway 55, at the stop sign next to the Mexican restaurant, that we heard all the sirens and stopped while the police cars and and the fire truck hurried past us and headed in the direction we were going.

"Must be something awful," I said to Ledford, who rolled down his window and waved at the men in the fire truck.

"Nah, around here, doesn't have to be anything to get that much attention. Probably a fight in the trailer park or a horse stuck in the electric fence. If it were bigger than that, the Tennessee patrollers would be crossing over."

He turned up the volume on his radio. It was a country music station, a song about a woman leaving town with her daughter. Ledford knew all the words.

"Lucas Boyd and his wife, Rhonda, own the campground, but they got an Asian woman running it. Her and Rhonda's mama. Lucas likes to run up and down the river. They're gone a lot."

Another police car sped past us as Ledford slowly pulled back onto the road and turned left at the signs for the campground.

"It's a nice place out here. Some developer from Nashville wanted to buy it last year, but Lucas wouldn't sell. He thinks campers ought to have a good place to vacation, too. Not just the rich people."

With all the fancy campers and trailer homes I had seen in the magazines and on the interstate, I wondered why Lucas Boyd and Ledford seemed to think that it wasn't rich people staying in campgrounds; but I guess they were right. Camping is a poor man's holiday. Or for me, a poor woman's life.

My travel trailer is a seventeen-foot Casita, a simple laid-up fiberglass design with a double-size bed, a table with captain chairs, a small bathroom, and a kitchen that has a two-eyed stove, a sink, a microwave, and a nice-sized refrigerator. Rip and I drove to Rice, Texas, to the manufacturing and distribution center about five years ago when we dreamed of weekends at the beach and when I still slept curved within his warm body, perfectly still, perfectly at ease with the place where I lay.

Over the five years of motor-home ownership, we went camping only four times, including the two nights in Texas after we bought the camper. That time we stayed at Grapevine Lake, near the airport, outside of Dallas. I cooked fish on the propane stove while he signed all the warranty cards and walked around and around the rig, trying to figure out where you attach the sewer hose. Both nights we crawled into bed, laughing at how uncomfortable it was without a good mattress and how he bumped his head every time he rolled over.

I had taken an extra job on the weekends working a shift in the emergency room and sold some of our furniture to buy our little vacation house on wheels. And even though I was entitled to more than what I got from the divorce settlement, after the long year of fighting and losing and after almost twenty years of marriage, all I wanted was that camper.

All I wanted was a chance to get away and belong to something that I could think of as mine. In spite of the fact there were a few memories lodged in the carpeted corners of that little trailer, tucked inside the tiny compartments and folded in the stacks of towels under the bed, it was the one place, the one thing that we both knew he never really wanted. It was the one thing we both agreed was completely mine.

The other things—the house, a newly remodeled ranch-style built in a clearing off the main road from Rocky Mount to Battleboro, oak wood paneling and new ceramic tile in the kitchen;

the dining-room table and chairs, dark cherry, smooth as skin; the hideaway bed we kept for the company that never came; even the lawn furniture that I picked out from some fancy catalog I found at the beauty parlor and had delivered while he was away at a business conference—everything we had was all somehow ours, belonging to the two of us, shared property, combined ownership.

After seeing him sitting in that restaurant, all leaned over across the table, holding that girl's long delicate hands, whispering something that made her blush and drop her face away from him, her blond hair cascading down her shoulders and draped over her pink cheeks, the grin unbroken and spread across his splendid face, after seeing all that played out before me like some bigger-than-life Technicolor movie, I desired nothing that bore resemblance to who I thought we were.

The trailer that he considered too small for the marriage, too small for the two of us together, was all I said I wanted.

As we got ready to take the turn into the campground, where a big wooden sign marked the entrance to Shady Grove, an ambulance pulled around us and suddenly it seemed as if Ledford had become interested in all the commotion.

"You want to go see?" he asked as if we were old friends out for an afternoon ride.

I shrugged because at that point I was in no hurry, and he turned off his signal and followed the vehicle down the paved road that twisted and curved into gravel and finally ended right at the banks of the Mississippi River.

When he stopped his truck and killed the engine, I got out, and without speaking to each other, we both started walking toward the police officers, the firemen, and the recently arrived emergency medical technicians.

It seemed like I was on duty, as if I had been called from the hospital to assist some injured citizen. I felt the stares of a few policemen as Ledford walked over to the group standing near the squad car. I heard them greet one another as I inched a little closer to where the ambulance was parked. Once I saw what was happening, the recovery of a dead man from the water, I knew there wasn't anything a nurse could do.

I folded my arms across my chest and watched as the EMTs, a young muscular man and a woman, about twenty-five, got out of the vehicle and walked over to the body. It was completely out of the river. As the woman knelt by the victim's head, I noticed the way she turned and looked away. I assumed there was a stench.

She stood up and tucked her head beside her shoulder, and the two paramedics returned to the ambulance. I figured they were going to get the black plastic body bag.

One of the policemen, the sheriff, I think, walked over, placed a handkerchief across his face, and appeared to make a positive identity. He said something to one of the deputies who had joined him, and the two of them laughed quietly while they glanced around nervously.

I saw the dead man as he lay on the bank. He was wearing a suit or what was left of one, the jacket ripped, the pants torn, his feet bare, the current of the river probably yanking off his shoes and socks. I couldn't make out his features, only noticed that he was dark-skinned.

It was easy to say, however, even from as far away as I stood, even as a group of policemen and firemen gathered around the victim, just from how the body lay upon that riverbank, crumpled and still, that he was dead.

The two emergency medical technicians were standing at the ambulance taking out what they needed when Ledford walked over to where I was waiting. We watched as a few of the men went to the vehicle and stood talking to the two paramedics as they unfolded the body bag.

"Drowning," the truck driver said, as if I needed an explanation.

I nodded.

"Anybody you know?" I asked.

"Funeral director," he answered. "From south side," he added, as if I should know what that meant. "Been missing a couple of days."

He shook his head and looked out across the river. "We find a lot of 'em out here," he said, and although I wasn't sure I knew what he meant, I nodded my head as if I understood exactly what he was saying.

"Well, I guess we've seen enough," he noted.

We both turned and walked back to his truck and got in.

He whipped around the large grassy lot, waved at the policemen, and as we passed him, I noticed the stare of the sheriff in my direction. Ledford pulled out onto the paved road and turned down the entrance to the campground. We drove a couple hundred yards and he stopped.

"Here's the office," he said, pointing with his chin over to a small log cabin situated on the left side.

There was a narrow porch with one chair in the middle and an ice machine pushed against the back wall. The OPEN sign was swinging across the window in the door and a hummingbird darted along the top ledge from one feeder to the next.

"Tell her you want a river view," he said as he pulled a pack of gum from his front pocket and held it out to me as an offer. "The sites in the woods are cooler, but the bugs are bad."

I smiled and declined the gum. I stepped out of his truck and walked inside. A small Asian woman was talking on the phone. She quickly ended her conversation and put the receiver down in its cradle. She glanced up at me and then out the window at the camper.

"Dead man," she said, shaking her head. "Found him washed up about a half a mile upriver."

I nodded, but didn't explain that I had just seen the body. I figured it would sound odd that we had stopped up the river to watch them pull the man out before I checked in.

"Bad luck for campground," she added.

She looked out the window again and noticed Ledford driving the truck. She waved at him. He nodded in recognition. Then she turned back to me as if trying to size up the situation.

"Two adults?" she asked.

"No, he's just brought me out here." I thought this sounded suspicious so I explained. "My car broke down. It's at the gas station on I-Forty. This gentleman was kind enough to tow me out here."

She studied me. "How many nights?"

"I'm not sure," I answered. "I guess just one."

"Jimmy Novack?" she asked.

I didn't know what she meant. She waited.

"The gas station. It a Chevron? Jimmy Novack's station?"

"Oh," I replied. "Yes, it was a Chevron station."

"Three nights, four days at least," she said, reaching across the desk and handing me a form. "Just fill out the top part."

"Four days? Really?" I asked. "I don't think it's that much of a problem, just a hose or belt of some kind. I've never had to leave my vehicle for three nights with a mechanic."

"Four days," she responded. "Jimmy Novack always take four days."

I sighed, figuring there was no reason to argue with her, filled out the form, and handed her my Visa credit card. She slid it through the machine and I watched nervously to see if it still worked.

I had asked Rip not to cancel that card until I could get settled. It was the one credit card I kept, thinking I might need it after I decided to leave North Carolina. It was also the only card that I had been using for more than six years since I was trying to earn points toward a trip to Paris for the two of us to share on our twentieth anniversary. It was going to be a surprise.

We were only 9,000 points short when I noticed on a monthly statement that we had received a bonus of 1,500 points when we stayed at the Marriott Hotel in Raleigh, a special offer for Visa card members. I knew I had never stayed at the Marriott Hotel in Raleigh, and I knew that the date recorded on the statement was the weekend Rip was supposed to be in Florida, at some car race with his brother.

It wasn't long after that, that I spotted him in the restaurant with that girl. Me staring through the window like some hungry orphan. The waiter suddenly looking up from the table at me as if he recognized my disappointment. The slow motion acknowledgment of a lie. After that, I quit counting the points and I never read the statements.

A few months later the UPS man delivered a new set of luggage, that expensive kind with thick brown leather, the kind with the name embroidered on the strip beneath the handle. Rip had ordered three pieces as a reward for using that Visa card. He said that he thought he could use them on his business trips, that he saw them in the magazine and ordered them for us.

I never told him about the surprise vacation I was planning or the way I had been using that card so carefully, counting the points like a child adding up her coins, day after day. I never told him that I expected that he would love me for twenty years and that I thought we'd order wine and cheese using the French words I had learned from cassette tapes and dance beneath summer stars all alone on one of the little bridges that passed over the Seine.

I never told him anything about what I knew or didn't know. I just asked him to let me use the card until I could open up my own line of credit.

The machine hummed and spat out the receipt and the woman behind the counter yanked it out and placed it in front of me to sign. Then she took out a map and pointed to the site she had chosen for me. It was a nice pull-through, with full hookup, 30 amp, water, sewer, even cable for the television. It was the last site on the river row, number 76.

"Pets on leash," she added as I turned toward the door, "and leave your garbage on the picnic table. I pick it up every morning."

I opened the door. "Thank you," I said as I walked out onto the porch.

"Ledford will show you everything." I heard the laughter in her voice.

I closed the door behind me. The phone had started to ring. I got back into the truck and pulled the door closed.

"You get a river site?" he asked as he turned down the volume on the radio.

"Number Seventy-six," I replied.

"Oh, that's a good one," he said as he pulled his truck into gear. "You got a whole side to yourself."

He drove ahead on the gravel road and then turned right on a dirt path toward the Mississippi River. There was a long row of campers only about fifty feet from the bank. He turned left and drove to the end of the row. He was right. It was a nice spot.

He pulled through and stopped and we both got out. As he started to unhook the camper from the hitch, I stood outside and stared across the river. It was brown and moving fast. Pieces of driftwood hurried by as water swirled and capped in small white waves.

A barge was stopped and docked across the river at a long, sandy island. To the right, downstream, around a curve, I could still see flashing lights and small groups of people huddled together. I thought about what I had just seen, a dead man lifted from the arms of the muddy water.

"You know how to get everything connected?" Ledford asked as he unchained the final hitch that held us together. He was in a squatted position, bent over the connection between his vehicle and my travel trailer.

I turned around and walked to the rear of his truck. I nodded. I learned everything about hooking and unhooking before I left North Carolina.

I watched as Ledford slowly cranked and released the ball of his trailer hitch from the attachment on the camper. He pushed my camper slightly away from his truck and tightened the chain around the long silver bar and then reattached the lock, pulling the two ends together.

"There," he said and stood up admiring his work, sliding his hands down the front of his pants. "You're all disconnected."

He looked at his watch. "You sure you don't need any more help?" he asked, eyeing me to see if I really knew how to set up camp.

"No, I'm good," I answered.

I figured he wanted to get out of there and go fishing and I suddenly thought that maybe I should offer him some money for the service he had provided. I went back around to the truck and retrieved my purse. Ledford walked to the river and stared down toward the spot where everyone had gathered, the spot where we had just been, the scene of the recovery.

"Dang," he said, as if he had just thought about it. "I bet that means they close Parker's Road."

He walked to where I was standing.

"I really appreciate you helping me." I reached inside my purse for my wallet. "I'd be happy to pay you for your trouble."

I knew my cash was low, and even though I was sincere in my offer, I was hopeful he'd decline.

He did.

"Nah," he answered as he opened his door and got in. "No trouble." And he started his engine.

"By the way," he said as he shifted into gear and stepped on the brake. "I never asked you what your name is or where you were going."

He turned to face me as I stood just a few feet from his truck.

I waited a minute, watching the river run past.

"Rose Franklin," I said, using only my first and middle name, my mother's maiden name, just trying it out to see how it sounded. "And here," I added, just like I knew it was meant to be. "I was going here."

He grinned and raised his chin at me. "Well, then, Ms. Rose Franklin, I'm glad I was able to get you where you needed to be."

He stuck his arm out the window, his elbow bent and resting on the frame of the door. "This is a good place."

And he held up his hand in a wave of good-bye, pulled

away from my trailer, cut the corner, and drove out of the campground.

I watched the dust lift and settle behind him, and then I turned back around to study the narrow stretch of muddy water that a man I never knew, a man who shared the same name as my mother, a man by the name of Lawrence Franklin V, had chosen as his place to die.

THE SECOND DAY

Roll on down, Sister
Roll on down.
Judgment Day here
The lost been found.

Roll on down, Sister
Roll on down.
Freedom's for sale
We Gloryland bound

Roll on down, Sister
Roll on down.
Bring my love
To the resting ground.

Roll on down, Sister
Roll on down.

TWO

The sun was high and bright by the time I awoke the next morning. I rolled out of bed and immediately thought of food.

It had taken me longer than I had expected to get my travel trailer set up after being delivered to the site by Ledford. By the time the sun went down I had everything completed, but I was tired and fell asleep immediately, getting up only once during the night sometime just after a storm had rolled through.

I had filled up my refrigerator with food in North Carolina, but I had not eaten since breakfast on the day of my arrival to West Memphis. I was hungry.

I went quickly to relieve myself in my little toilet, brushed my teeth, splashed water on my face, and then fixed a peanut butter sandwich, sliced an apple, poured a glass of milk, opened the blinds by the table, and sat down to eat.

A few folks were walking along the path by the river. Two little girls were playing near an old landing, a small patch of ground with a single tree fixed upon it. One girl was bent down, near the tree, picking up rocks or pieces of trash and placing them near the other one who sat on the bench, swinging a long, crooked branch from the tree.

Outside my window, straight ahead at the motor home next to mine, a police officer was talking to a couple standing near the gravel drive. I couldn't hear the conversation. I could only see that the man was shaking his head while the woman shielded her eyes with her hand, watching the two girls. The officer was taking notes.

I finished my sandwich, cleaned up after myself, changed into shorts and a T-shirt, and was making the bed when I heard a knock at my door. I peeked out the window and saw that it was the policeman I had just seen who was talking to the people staying next to me. I opened the door.

"Excuse me, ma'am," he said, pulling out the word *ma'am* with a long drawl. "Don't mean to bother you."

I smiled. "No bother."

I stepped out from the doorway and landed in front of the officer, who moved a few steps back, giving me room.

I was glad I was dressed, glad I had eaten and managed to appear prepared for the day, for visitors, for questions. As I moved outside, I noticed that the couple from next door was now watching me and that the two little girls had stopped playing and were looking in my direction.

Suddenly, I felt guilty and began to sense the race in my pulse that seemed to happen any time I encountered a policeman.

The officer was young, maybe mid-twenties, tanned and

muscular. His navy blue uniform was freshly ironed, starched, and a perfect fit. He spoke politely, professionally. I assumed he was new in this line of work, that he was just learning how to conduct himself in an interview, that he was clearly following protocol, going completely by the book.

As I tried masking all signs of guilt, reminding myself that I had done nothing wrong, I wondered if he would be different in five or ten years. If he would still iron and starch his uniform, if he would continue using such politeness when he spoke. If the things he had been taught in the beginning about courtesy and the goodness in human nature, if these things would continue to matter to him, if he would still hold them as true.

I studied the young man in front of me, slowed my breathing, and decided I had nothing to be afraid of. I had no reason to be nervous.

"I'm Deputy Fisk," he said as he pulled out a business card and handed it to me. "I'm interviewing everybody staying at the campground to find out who was here this weekend."

He glanced over my shoulder, examining the side of my camper. He seemed to be making notes in his mind.

"Yes, sir," I answered, even though he was at least fifteen years younger than I. Old habits are hard to break. "I just arrived yesterday."

He took off his sunglasses and placed them in his front pocket and took out a small notepad. His eyes were dark brown, kind, unassuming.

"Okay." He clicked his pen and began to write. "Do you mind if I ask your name and where you're from?"

JACKIE LYNN

I shook my head.

"Rose Franklin," I said, not knowing why, but feeling comfortable now in my choice to drop my husband's name and my father's as well. "And I'm from North Carolina."

He kept writing. Then he stopped and looked up at me. His whole face a question mark.

"Something wrong?" I asked.

He shook his head and wrote another note or two in his pad.

"This about the drowned man?" I asked. I didn't remember the deputy from the group of officers I had seen the day before, but I assumed the death had prompted the questioning of everyone near the scene.

He nodded. "Apparent suicide. But we need to ask around, you know, just to be sure—" He stopped. "You know, since it happened at the river and everything."

I didn't know.

"I drove over and saw all the commotion yesterday." I turned toward where I had seen the cars and lights below the campground.

"Yes, ma'am." He followed my eyes. "That's where we found the body, but the sheriff thinks he went in somewhere upriver."

He turned, glancing to his left, his eyes facing all the way to Memphis. "It was farther up than here."

It was as if he were talking to himself, making his presumption out loud, so I didn't respond.

"Well." He turned again to me. "It doesn't sound like you could know anything since you just got to town." He hesitated a moment, perhaps making sure that he shouldn't ask me any-thing else.

"Thanks for your time." He put his sunglasses on and put the little notebook and the pen in his pocket.

I waited.

"What makes you figure it was suicide?" I asked, not sure he would tell me, not sure he should tell me since I had no real business in asking the question.

He folded his arms across his chest, relaxed slightly.

"Just the usual signs," he said easily. "Depression, the victim had just started some medication. Drew up a new will, wrote a letter, visited his loved ones, gave away all his stuff."

Right then, I thought about my last week in Rocky Mount and how, except for the medication part, my last few days in North Carolina looked exactly like the dead man's in West Memphis.

I recalled how I had made a special trip to Wilson to see a lawyer, one the divorce attorney told me about, and how I changed my will to take Rip out of it. I named my niece, Teensy, as the beneficiary of my insurance policy and then I just de-cided to make it simple and leave her everything, not that I had that much anyway. But the meager bit I had, I left to her because she's twenty and a little lost, reminds me of myself. I figured she needed the money more than anybody.

Then later I wrote a letter, but never delivered it. It was the story of how Rip and I fell away, how I felt wronged and broken, how I couldn't stay in the same town with him and his new wife.

It wasn't written to anybody in particular, just a means to say what was in my heart, a way to tell my truth. I don't know why I did it and afterward, I felt silly and exposed, so I tore it up and threw it away in the last bag of garbage that I left at the curb for pickup.

Then I saw my brother and his wife, shared a meal with them, and told them I was leaving town for a while. I went to the nursing home to visit my dad. I told him who I was three or four times, tried to make him understand that I wouldn't be coming back, that I wasn't his wife or his mother, but his daughter, and that I couldn't stay around anymore. He fell asleep while I tried to explain, so finally, I just kissed him on the forehead and walked away.

And I took two carloads of junk, clothes and knickknacks, records and picture frames, pillows and books, lamps, bowls, and plates to Goodwill. I sorted and saved and then sorted again, ending up giving or throwing away most of everything.

The truth is, I realized after listening to Deputy Fisk, I'd be lying if I said I didn't consider taking my own life, too. I'd be lying if I didn't confess that in the packing and the good-byes and the leaving and the sorting and the writing and the emptying, I didn't think it might all be better if instead of driving somewhere far away, I just took a handful of those pills that I had in my medicine cabinet or borrowed my brother's shotgun from his garage or just drove my car straight into the path of an eighteen-wheeler. Because the truth is, I did think about it. I did consider ending my own life, since I already felt dead inside anyway.

I almost killed myself like the drowned man. I almost decided that dying was easier than living, that suddenly nothing was very interesting to me except what might lie on the other side, what might await me after I took my last breath. Didn't even concern me that it might be judgment or darkness or punishment.

I still don't know what kept me from going ahead with it, how it was I got saved from myself and my brokenness. I'm convinced that it wasn't any of my own doing. And it caused me to think about the dead man and why it was he went ahead and did the thing I could not.

I cleared my mind of the thoughts of what I'd almost done.

"Why did you say what you did about the river?" I asked, recalling something he had mentioned earlier in the conversation.

He raised his eyebrows, tilted his head a bit as if he didn't know what I was asking.

I explained. "Why does it seem like it might not be suicide because of where it happened? Because of the river?"

"Oh, that." He understood then why I asked. He remembered his previous comment.

He dropped his arms to his side, stepped back, and pitched one foot against the picnic table behind him.

"Just a lot of past sins in that river," he said, like somebody who had read all the books or heard all the stories, somebody who lived here and knew everybody, everything, by name.

"This end of it runs pretty fast all the way to the Gulf." He smiled and then added, "You can bury a lot in that muddy water," as if that somehow cleared up the intentions of what he had said.

I didn't say anything, but I knew what he meant. I had seen enough mob stories on television to know about dumping bodies in lakes and rivers.

"You didn't know the man, did you?"

He stood up, straight and at attention, and seemed to be studying me, but it was hard to tell with him wearing those dark sunglasses.

I was surprised by the question, shaking my head before I spoke. "No, I didn't know him. I told you I'm not from here," I added, suspicious of his query.

And then I had to ask. "Why do you think I would know him?"

He shifted his weight from side to side, watching me, sizing me up.

"Your last name," he answered, not realizing that it was my middle name, my mother's name. "It's the same as his."

He pulled at his belt, his chest widened. "Franklin," he said. "His name was Lawrence Franklin."

And somehow the news both stunned me and made me sad, kept me from telling the man that it wasn't even really my last name. I just shook my head as if I were making some confession, like the sound of my denial could make his death even harder.

"No," I replied in earnest. "I didn't know him."

Just then a golf cart swung around the corner and stopped right in front of us. It was the Asian woman I had met at the office the day before, when I checked in, the manager. She had been picking up trash.

"You bother my guests?" she asked Deputy Fisk and smiled, though it hardly seemed pleasant or real.

"No, Mary, I'm just following orders." He smiled back at her, his gesture seeming more genuine.

"He bothering you?" she asked me, as if his response was unreliable. She waited to see how I would reply.

I shook my head. "No, he's just asking me about the man who drowned."

She made a hissing noise and threw up her hands. "She not even here until yesterday. Why you not stop by my office and ask me who was here and who was not?" She was clearly annoyed.

"I did stop by, but nobody was there." He spoke slowly in defense of himself, carefully, using a low and easy tone.

"You could wait. I was gone for only ten minutes." She popped the brake in the cart and pushed the gear into reverse.

"You come to the office and I'll give you report."

And she drove away without even a greeting of farewell or picking up the garbage off the picnic tables farther down the row of campers.

There was a pause as the dust lifted and fell around us.

I raised my eyes to the officer.

"It doesn't seem as if she cares very much for your presence here." I sat down on the step.

He laughed. "She's just very protective of her campers." He looked at his watch. "There's some history here."

He tapped at the middle of his sunglasses and my curiosity was aroused at his suggestion about Shady Grove, that there was some police history, some criminal history, something that involved having a deputy at the campground. I wanted to ask what he meant, but I had heard about the code of silence among law officials. I knew I had already surpassed my limit of acceptable questions for a policeman. I didn't ask anything else.

"Well, thank you, Ms. Franklin, for your time. I hope you enjoy your stay in West Memphis."

He started to walk to his car that was parked at the other end of the campground. "By the way"—he turned back around—"how long you planning to stay?"

"I don't know." I answered. "Awhile, maybe."

I stood up straight and looked over the river, trying on my new name, trying on this new residence. "I sort of like it here."

He smiled, surprising me with his good nature. "Fine. Then stay for as long as you can. It's real pretty out here, especially in the fall."

I stood at my door and watched as the young officer of the law turned, walked to his car, and drove away.

THREE

After the deputy left, I went inside and put on a pair of flip-flops and a hat. I decided that since my cell phone wasn't charged that I should go to the office and use the phone there, try to find out if the mechanic was able to fix my car. And I thought I might enjoy a walk around the campground, the chance to see more of the place, more of this site where I was now known as my mother's child, Rose Franklin.

I stepped outside, closed the camper door, and started to my left. I walked down to the river, where there was a parallel set of long steel rails that had been broken in several places. They appeared as if at one time they had been the means by which folks walked down from the bank and into the river, though now they were unconnected and unsteady. There was a concrete landing that stretched from the broken railings all the way down past the tree where the two young girls were still playing.

The river rushed by, away from Memphis, away from the two

interstates. It was high along the bank, slapping against the concrete and pushing wildly down to the south. I stood near the railings and wondered about Mr. Franklin and how it was that he had decided to die in this way, how it was that he was able to walk or dive or allow himself to be pushed into the river and drown.

I had always heard that drowning was a violent way to die, that since it is a natural reflex to fight the flow of water into the lungs, a natural reflex to grasp and pull for breath, a drowning victim is a person who dies in panic. I figured that the dead man would have to have been drunk or drugged in some way, a means to slow down that reflex to take a breath. Or maybe, I thought, he strapped something to himself, a weighted object, a cement block or a bag of rocks, something that he wouldn't be able to fight against, something to weigh himself down with.

Then I guessed that if he was considering suicide, made all the arrangements, that more than likely, his burden may have been enough. That the sorrow or the grief or the disappointment was heavy enough or big enough or complicated enough that he didn't have to strap anything to his chest, that he didn't have to manufacture the weight, that all he had to do was fall into the river and that the trouble around his heart would steal away both his natural urge and his ability to fight for air.

I slid off my flip-flops and leaned down, holding on to one of the railings, hoping that it might be sturdy enough to balance me. I knelt down easily, and let the river flow through my fingers; when I felt the water pass through, I knew.

This water would have taken the man's sacrifice gladly. It would have let him walk down, press his face into the current, and then sailed him right out and away, past any safety. Feeling it there, pushing through my flesh, I was sure about the Mississippi. It was clearly that relentless.

"Hey, you should be careful."

It was a child's voice, speaking behind me. I glanced up and around.

"It's slippery."

She was no more than nine or ten, waiting at the edge of the grass. She was one of the girls I had seen playing earlier, the one gathering things from around the tree, presenting them to the other one who sat near her on the bench.

"Yes, I know," I answered, standing up and twisting around to face her.

Using the bar, I pulled myself back to where she was. "And these things don't seem too reliable." I meant, of course, the broken rails.

I stood next to her, putting on my flip-flops, facing the river.

The little girl was skinny. Her soft brown hair was plaited into tiny braids that ended in brightly colored barrettes all across her head. She was as light as brown sugar and she was wearing pink shorts and a clean white T-shirt with a pink flower right in the center. She squinted her eyes up at me.

"That policeman talk to you?" she asked. She had a flower stem in her hand, twirling it around.

"Yes, he did," I answered. I looked around to see if his car was gone.

"He talked to my mom and dad, too," she replied. "But he didn't ask me anything."

I nodded and wondered if she had an answer that was just waiting for the right question. I knew that often the police over-look young witnesses, operating under clear prejudices that children don't know anything. Turns out, I've learned, they know a lot more than one thinks.

"Somebody died here a couple of days ago." She flung the green stem in the air. "So it must be really dangerous."

"I think you're right," I answered.

"Where are you from?" she asked, turning to look at my camper.

"North Carolina," I said. "And you?"

"We're from Kentucky." She picked up the narrow stem again and flung it. "My sister's here to see a doctor."

She pointed toward the other little girl, still sitting on the bench beside the tree where they had been playing. "She's been sick a long time."

I glanced in the girl's direction and nodded again. Her sister was facing forward, watching the barges or the river or whatever it was right before her. She had not moved from where she had been previously, the first time I noticed her.

"Well, I'm sorry to hear that." I wasn't sure how to respond. "I hope this doctor will help her."

"I don't think so," she replied quickly, and I wondered if she had overheard her parents' pessimism or if she had come to this conclusion on her own.

I didn't ask for an explanation.

"We've been here almost a week."

I swatted at a few gnats that were crawling up my leg. The sun was getting hot and I wished I had put on some lotion.

"Do you like camping here?" I asked.

"It's okay," she answered. "There's not much to do after we have to go to the hospital." She sat down on the grass. "But I'm used to that."

I waited and then sat down next to her, my legs stretching far beyond hers. "My name is Rose," I said, introducing myself.

"I'm Clara," she replied. "That's Jolie"—she motioned with her chin toward her sister—"She's older than me."

"Well, Clara," I said, "It's very nice to meet you."

She smiled. "You have any children?"

I shook my head.

"You not want any children?" she asked.

"No, just had some problems." After more than ten years of disappointment, the words I chose for explanation fell more easily.

"I'm giving blood for my sister." She swept her hands across the grass between us.

I nodded and leaned back against my elbows, pulling up my knees and feet.

"That's very brave of you," I said in a tone of congratulation. "That's a very nice thing to do for your sister."

"I guess," she answered. "I have to be really careful all the time so I don't get hurt."

She picked up a small stone and threw it in the river, then she drew her legs in, crossing them at the ankles. She reached out and took hold of her feet and I noticed the bruises up and down her arms. She bent forward, touching her forehead to her feet.

"I can swim," she reported. "But not in there." She glanced at the river. "It's too fast."

"Plus there's all the boats," I replied, watching as a couple of barges were coming upstream. "And it seems a little muddy."

She nodded.

"You can swim in the ponds," she said, turning her head.

I glanced behind us. There were two big ponds, one directly behind the last row of campers and another on the other side of the campground entrance. Suddenly, I remembered having seen a small red light the night before when I got up to change into my pajamas and close the blinds, the one time I had gotten up all night.

Just as I had pulled the cord I had looked out toward the pond and seen a tiny ember, the end of a cigarette. I figured the smoker was simply standing outside, away from his camper. I didn't even think to notice what time it was.

"You just have to watch for snakes." She fell back, placing her arms behind her head. She was staring up at the sky.

I pulled my knees to my chest, leaning my head back. There were a few clouds overhead, thin summer ones, only a slight threat of rain. We sat like that for a while without talking.

"He wasn't sad like they say." She was staring straight above her head, as if the words she was saying were written in the sky.

I wasn't sure who she meant, what story she was telling, so I just watched the clouds as well and let her go on.

"He was singing and laughing."

I faced her.

"Who?" I asked. "Who was singing?"

"The man in the river," she answered. "The one they found, down at the sandbar." She sat up and began pulling out the grass that had gotten stuck in her hair.

Just then, the woman in the camper beside mine stood outside on the front step, calling for the little girl. "Clara!" she yelled. "Clara, time to go."

Slowly she got up beside me. She stood for a moment, not leaving. Her shoulders fell and a measure of resolve settled across her face.

"We got to go to the hospital now. I have to give some more blood."

I stood up beside her, trying to decide if I should ask her something else or if I should walk with her and tell her parents what she had just told me. I hesitated.

"Well, Clara," I said, still trying to make up my mind, "it was nice to meet you. I hope we'll see each other again later."

She turned away.

"Yep," was all she said as she headed toward the bench where her sister was sitting.

I watched her walk and wondered what would be the right thing to do. I couldn't decide if I should call Deputy Fisk and tell him that the little girl had seen the man before he drowned or if I should speak to her mother first. I thought that if I hurried, I might catch him before he left the office and I thought that if I moved quickly over there to let him know what she had just told me, he might speak to her or her parents before they left.

I watched her closely from where I was standing, trying to figure out what to do.

She lifted her sister. I saw the strength it took, the slim band of muscle stretching from her shoulder to her wrist, the way she bit her lip, positioned her legs, trying not to stumble, the easy but trusting way her sister wrapped her arm around the younger sibling.

I turned toward the camper and saw the mother's deep sigh as she closed and locked the door, the single strand of hair that slipped from her barrette and fell across her eyes.

The father came from behind their vehicle, a tall man, slightly hunched, pulling out the wheelchair from the rear of the van, the knowing way he opened it, spreading out the vinyl seat, wiping it with the open palm of his brown hand.

I watched as he pushed it near his two daughters and how Clara, the young one, knelt before her father and the chair and how he pulled his oldest child into himself, into the chair, with such tenderness.

I watched the way the family got ready to go to the hospital. The gentle but firm way they all carried the burden of one another. I saw the heaviness and the lightness, the loss and the gain, the unspoken way of waiting for good news but preparing for bad; I decided they didn't need to be bothered.

Maybe the little girl, Clara, saw the man before he died. Maybe she watched him speak his peace, say his prayers, sing his farewell; maybe no one else will ever know.

I decided as I watched the van pull out from the parking spot, the family huddled together inside, that what was over was over. And the dead man, regardless of what a child saw or didn't see, was still dead.

I pulled my hat over my eyes and slowly walked toward the path that wound around to the office, hoping that Deputy Fisk had left, planning only to use the phone and call the mechanic about my car. It did not seem fitting or significant to break the little girl's confidence, I decided as I walked.

I watched as they drove away. Clara rolled down the window at the backseat of the van, threw out her hand, and waved.

FOUR

Mary, it turns out, was right. It was going to be four days until my car would be fixed, the mechanic said when I talked to him. A part had to be shipped from Texas or Florida or somewhere that took longer than overnight to get it to West Memphis.

Mary just rolled her eyes when I told her what he said.

"Always a part have to be shipped," she responded in her clipped English. "I think Jimmy just like to keep cars around his shop, make him look busy."

She was filling out some monthly report when I got to the office. Deputy Fisk had already left, and I was glad I didn't have to see him again that morning.

"He got no business talking to my campers," Mary said when I asked if he was gone. She answered like she owned the place and we were specifically under her care. "Police never around when you need them, always around when you don't."

I agreed because I had some notion of what she was saying and was just about to comment when the front door opened, and I was suddenly face-to-face with a man and a woman I was sure were going to rob us. I immediately wished that the deputy had stayed around.

"About time you came back," Mary said to the couple as they stood in the doorway. "Your place is falling apart."

And that's when I realized I was about to meet Lucas and Rhonda Boyd, the owners of Shady Grove.

I'm not a person who generally makes immediate judgments about others, but these two would make a blind man nervous.

Lucas Boyd stood six feet and six inches tall. He had a black beard that fell far below his chin and a head shaved clean. There were tattoos running up and down both arms, and he wore a dark T-shirt and tight blue jeans with tall black boots and a leather belt, even on the hottest day in summer. Broad-chested like a ballplayer, but looking more like a wrestler, he was the kind of man Rip liked to make fun of, call Biker Boy or Cave Dweller.

He walked into that office and I almost fell off the stool I was sitting on. He was just that big, just that frightening. And when Rhonda Boyd stepped in behind him, flaming red hair pulled back in a bandana, leather jacket and dark shades, just as tattooed, just as threatening, almost as big, I knew right away what Fisk intended when he said the campground had "history" with the police.

Although I am a woman who tries to keep an open mind when I am being introduced to someone, I couldn't help but jump to conclusions upon meeting Lucas and Rhonda. They were exactly the kind of folks you think of when you hear the words "menace to society." Exactly the people you wouldn't want knowing your credit card number and your address.

Before I even knew who they were or the things of which they had been arrested and convicted of, I was convinced that they were running drugs up and down the river, that they both carried knives and guns, and that they killed puppies for sport. I was hiding my jewelry and pulling as far away from them as I could get.

I learned later that I wasn't the only one who bore these notions about the couple. They had been out of prison for more than twenty years when I met them, married and both of them demonstrating clean records for all that time, but unfortunately, I discovered the West Memphis police don't believe in rehabilitation.

They were also highly suspicious of the Boyds because the campground in West Memphis was known throughout the Arkansas prison system as a place where an ex-con can go and find a friendly face, get a second chance.

I had already seen a couple of shady-looking characters that morning mowing grass and cleaning out the showers. I knew that there are always a lot of chores to do at a campground and I guessed Lucas and Rhonda found a cheap labor source. However, with the looks of these two and the looks of some of the folks hanging out at Shady Grove, a person had to wonder right along with the sheriff and his deputies what really was going on along the western shore of the Mississippi River.

That first day I met them, and as I slowly moved near the rear of the office, Lucas walked in, smiling just like a Girl Scout. "How you doing there, little sister?"

I've now learned that Lucas calls all women under forty, "little sister," and all those past middle age, "dear," as in "dear sister."

"I'm just fine, thank you." I answered politely.

"Rose, this is Lucas," Mary introduced us just as Rhonda walked in. "And this is Rhonda, his wife," she added.

Rhonda nodded as she pulled off the bandana and tied her red hair back in a ponytail.

"Well, little sister Rose, it's a pleasure to meet you." Lucas moved toward me and stuck out his hand, and though I was nervous, I shook it. "You staying with us at Shady Grove?"

"She at number Seventy-six. Travel trailer," Mary answered for me.

Rhonda looked out the small window of the door, but I knew that you really couldn't see the river row from the office. She whipped around to face me. "Where's your car?" she asked and I wondered what else she saw, if she had a longer line of vision than most people.

"Pssst." Mary made that hissing noise she had made at Deputy Fisk. "Jimmy Novack got it."

Lucas grinned. "Four days." And he slapped me on the back like an old friend.

Rhonda walked around me and went behind the counter. "Mama still playing cards?"

Mary took a handful of papers and slipped them inside a

folder. She began straightening up around her. "I guess. She called and said she'd be here by lunchtime."

Rhonda moved over to the desk behind the counter while Lucas picked up the stack of mail, the newspaper, and sat down at a table pushed against the rear wall. He pulled out a small pair of glasses from the front pocket of his T-shirt and started reading.

"Rhonda's mother, Ms. Lou Ellen, plays cards at the Senior Center downtown," Mary said, as a way of introducing the absent woman to me. "She helps run the place, takes reservations, greets the guests, keeps up with the bookwork," she added while she opened and closed the drawer by her.

"But not in the mornings," Rhonda said. "In the mornings, Mama plays canasta and bridge and sometimes a hand or two of poker."

She sat down. "Mama is serious about her cards."

I smiled, trying to seem relaxed.

"Well, it looks like they're still waiting for the report from the autopsy of Mr. Franklin." Lucas was reading the paper and when he said the name, "Mr. Franklin," my head jerked in his direction.

It shocked me, is all. Hearing the name again like that. My mother's name in the same sentence as the word *autopsy*. Rhonda noticed my surprise. The other two in the room looked over at me.

"My name is Franklin," I said as a means of explaining, without completely explaining.

Both Lucas and Rhonda glanced at me and then at each other.

"Lawrence Franklin was the man they found yesterday up at the sandbar," Rhonda responded because she thought I didn't know.

I nodded. "Yes, the police officer told me his name. It just seemed weird hearing you say it like that."

"Who was it?" Lucas asked, meaning the police officer. I was confused at the time. He was staring at Mary, waiting for her answer.

"Same guy who came last month. Fisk," Mary said, sounding it out more like *fish* than what it was.

Lucas just shook his head while he turned the pages of the paper. "Well, I just pray for the dead man's soul and I trust in the mercy of our good Lord. That family and that river have both seen enough sorrow and sadness to last a thousand years." And he folded the paper and took off his glasses and bowed his head as if he were praying.

Rhonda and Mary bowed, too, and since I didn't know what else to do, I dropped my head as well.

Lucas said, "Amen," and Rhonda and Mary snapped up their heads and went back to work.

After the awkward brief moment of silence that I assumed was a prayer, I heard a car pull up. We all turned toward the door as an older man, smiling and nodding, walked in. Lucas introduced me to Mr. Clarence Broadnax, the deacon chairman from the Antioch Holiness Church, the same place, I was told, where Lawrence Franklin, the deceased, was also a member.

We smiled at each other, and I tried to think of a way to excuse myself; but there just didn't seem to be a polite way to exit.

Lucas and Mr. Broadnax talked about the weather and fishing until the conversation finally got around to the dead man, a mutual friend of both the visitor and the campground owner. The deacon was asked about Mr. Franklin's funeral. The older man dropped his head and reported that the preacher said he wouldn't hold the funeral at the church of a person who had committed suicide. He said the death was the work of the devil and he couldn't see bringing such evil into the sanctuary.

The deacon remained standing at the door, his hat in his hand, and just shook his head. "Don't seem right," he kept repeating. "Lawrence Franklin been with Antioch since he was a baby. His great-grandfather donated the land to build the building. And that family has done every funeral of every dead member of that church. Some of 'em for free. And now we're gonna turn our backs on this man."

He just shook his head.

"Lawrence would never do what they said he did," he noted. "He worked too hard to give it all up like that."

Lucas agreed.

"I just don't believe it either," Lucas said. "What could have been so terrible that happened to make a man do that?" he asked. "To make Mr. Franklin do that?" He clasped his hands together and placed them on the table in front of him.

"That's just it, he wouldn't do it," the deacon replied. "Lawrence Franklin had too much respect for life. He just wouldn't do it," he said again, this time his voice breaking from sorrow.

Mary shuffled her papers and moved things around on the

counter. Rhonda turned toward her husband as if he might offer some comfort. And I just looked away. I was embarrassed for him, revealing such emotion, bearing the vulnerability of his disappointment so openly in front of a stranger.

And then, taking the cue from his wife, Lucas spoke up. There was hardly even a hesitation, just time enough for the thought of it. "We'll have a service for Mr. Franklin here, by the river."

The rest of us stayed quiet. Imagining such a thing. Considering such an idea.

Lucas continued. "We'll rent one of those real nice tents and put it up right at the edge of the landing. The processional can drive upriver row. I'll explain everything to the other campers, and they can stay away if they want or they can participate. We'll have a nice dinner afterward and invite everybody."

He went on. "Mr. Franklin loved this river, came down here almost every day to check the current or measure the sediment or to fish in the pond. He went to see his Maker at the river. We might as well have his service here."

I thought it was about the craziest idea I had ever heard. A funeral at a campground? A memorial service down at the river? The river where the man died? A dinner for the family and campers? Just sounded nutty to me. But I guess I was the only one who thought so because I glanced up and both Mary and Rhonda were nodding their heads in agreement, a big grin stretched across Rhonda's face.

"Well," the deacon replied after a long pause. "I guess I'll have to ask Ms. Eulene about this. She is the mother of the deceased. And this is highly unusual."

I thought to myself, Well, that's an understatement if I've ever heard one. And I just knew the deacon would decline the offer. I mean, I figured he'd be polite about it, but I surely thought he'd speak for the family and the deacon board and for all folks sensible, and decline. But he didn't.

He tucked in his bottom lip, chewing on it a bit.

"I think it sounds real nice." He slid his fingers along the brim of his hat.

He spoke quietly. "You know we was baptized together in the river." He bowed his head. "Not too far from here," he added, then waited as if he was remembering.

"Serve that old back-stabbing preacher right. Lawrence and I both agreed years ago that we were closer to the Lord fishing than we were listening to Rev. Henley try to preach." He nodded. "Yes sir, I think it sounds just right."

As stunned as I was, I turned to see how Lucas was going to react. I guess I was still thinking it might be a joke or something, that he'd name some church that would be more fitting, that he'd offer another alternative. But he didn't. And to see the look on his face. It was almost holy.

I don't mean a look that was self-righteous or the kind to show that he was pleased with himself, I mean it was as if some glory shone on him. It was like a look I've never known, never seen, and in spite of the fear and doubt that had been raised in my mind about him and his wife, it did cause me to think that maybe there was something like the Kingdom of God down by that river.

The deacon talked a little more about the summer storms and the sorrow over the death in the south side community, how the death of Lawrence Franklin still left them shocked and cold. Then he said he had to be going and then not much later Rhonda and Lucas left, and then it was just Mary and me in the office, the way it was before they all came in.

She had a couple of phone calls to make while I studied the map of the United States they had posted on the wall, and then when she was finished talking on the phone, I asked her what she really thought about having a funeral at the campground.

She just waved her hand in front of her face. "Pssst." She made that noise she liked to make again. "That's nothing new for here."

I watched her, waiting for more.

"We have weddings, birthday parties, sobriety parties, homecoming parties, church revivals, and all kinds of reunion parties. Funeral, no big thing. Shady Grove always a place to mark great passage in life. It just like the river."

I didn't know what she meant at the time. I didn't even know that she was talking about the Mississippi River, the banks upon which this campground was founded. I just knew when I heard it, that it felt right what she was saying about Shady Grove. Sometimes a place just knows how to honor important moments. Sometimes a place takes up life inside itself and just knows how to mark a thing passed or completed or good.

I must admit, however, that at the time, I still had some difficulty in thinking about a funeral being held at a campground. I would never identify myself as a religious person and I don't have any particular opinions about the sacredness of a church building, but I just never considered taking death down to a river. I never thought about a service of memory being held at a place so open, so wild. I guess that's why I said what I did to Mary.

"Maybe the old man is right," I noted. "Maybe it wasn't suicide after all. And maybe if the preacher knew this, there wouldn't be a funeral by the river, they'd have the rightful service in the church."

Mary tilted her head to one side, handed me a real hard look. "Everybody say it's suicide," she said quietly.

"Maybe everybody doesn't know everything," I answered her.

"You police?" she asked, holding me with a stare.

"No," I answered. "I'm a nurse, but I know a few things." I smiled. "I'm just saying that things aren't always what they seem."

She blew out a long breath. "Yes. This fact I know for sure."

"Maybe the police just took the easiest answer, just assumed he had killed himself because of a few things they found out. Maybe they don't want to work too hard." I was sorting through possibilities.

"It could be a cover-up of some kind." And I began to think of other explanations of how a dead man rolled up on the banks of the Mississippi River. I thought about a boat accident and wondered if Mr. Franklin owned one.

I felt the office manager staring at me. I turned to her. My face gave away my question. "What?" I asked.

She kept watching me and finally posed the question that

was clearly bothering her. "Why you so interested in this man?" she asked.

The query was a good one, one I hadn't considered. I shrugged my shoulders. "I don't know," I replied.

I could tell my answer wasn't good enough for her.

"It just doesn't seem right," I noted. "I mean, it just feels like there's something else going on."

Mary still stared at me. I could tell she didn't believe me, so I thought about her question. I thought about the reason I was so concerned about a cause of death for a man I didn't know. I wondered why I was so intrigued by something I had nothing to do with.

"Maybe I just prefer to think about somebody else's tragedy for a while." I paused, realizing I was getting close to the truth.

"I left North Carolina to get away from things in my own life. Maybe I'm just finding it easier to focus on this dead man's trouble than it is to focus on mine right now," I confessed.

The woman nodded and looked away. I knew I had answered her question and had uncovered something very important for myself as well. I didn't have to say anything else.

And then, without either one of us knowing it at the time, she said the one sentence that would change my life forever.

"You should talk to Tom."

She said the words as if he was just some man from West Memphis, just some ordinary being who would report to me a bit of history or some legend, somebody, who at the time, we both expected would mean nothing more to me than the facts he could tell.

"Tom?" I asked.

"Tom Sawyer," she replied. She waited.

"Tom knew the dead man. They old friends, fish and hang out together a lot. He would know if it was suicide or not. Tom Sawyer would know."

And upon hearing his name, without having the time to guard my reaction, silence my disrespect, or recognize the fluttering of wings in my spirit, a door opened to my heart; I laughed out loud.

FIVE

Mary did not know the literary figure Tom Sawyer. She had never heard of Mark Twain or Huckleberry Finn, though she did think she had met a man named Jim. Mostly however, she did not understand why I would consider it as odd that a man who lived near the Mississippi River would have been given the name of Tom Sawyer.

"It's just funny," I said, "that a mother would choose to name her child after a boy from a book, especially a boy like Tom Sawyer."

"Why?" she asked. "This Tom Sawyer, he have demons?"

I shook my head.

"Bad blood?"

"No," I answered.

"Then, why it so strange?"

"It's just ironic. Two people living near the same area having the same name."

She shrugged her shoulders and suddenly didn't seem very interested anymore.

"Tom Sawyer." I was not finished trying to make her see the irony. "He was this little mischievous kid who was best friends with a boy who runs away with a slave."

No reaction from Mary.

"They live on the Mississippi River. He lives with his aunt Polly, wants to start up a band of robbers."

She rolled her eyes.

"It's just odd, don't you agree, that somebody living on the Mississippi River is named after somebody else who was supposed to live on the same river?"

She drew in a breath and yawned.

I don't know why now, but at that time it was really important that I make her understand me. "Can't you agree that it's just a little strange that two people with the same name wind up being in the same place?"

"Like you and Mr. Franklin," she said, and her observation stunned me.

There was a hesitation before I responded. I knew she remembered that I had registered as Rose Griffith, that my credit card had that name imprinted on it as well. I could tell that she was trying to figure out why I had lied.

"Yes, I guess, like me and Mr. Franklin."

I waited.

"Griffith is my married name. I'm divorced," I said, explaining. "Franklin isn't really my last name either."

She raised her eyes, interested, confused.

"It's my mother's name," I continued. "It's the one I've chosen."

"Rose Franklin, Lawrence Franklin. Tom Sawyer, Thomas Sawyer," she said it easily, but with much clarity.

And once it was said like that, our names the same, like two people called Tom Sawyer, somehow it instantly drew me to the dead man, tied us together forever, divided his burden, placing some of it squarely on my back.

At the time of this early revelation, of course, I was not able to articulate any of my vast emotions or my desire to understand the cause of death, as well as the precipitant events that occurred days or weeks before my arrival and before Mr. Lawrence Franklin's drowning. I just knew that our shared name was now a rope that tied me to the dead man, linking us together in a way I couldn't understand.

"Always more than how it seem," Mary said, reminding me of the earlier part of our conversation and pulling me back to the moment that was at hand.

"Yes," I agreed. "Always more."

She glanced up at the clock. "I have to go pick up trash again," she said, apparently finished with our discussion of names and characters. "First time through, not everybody ready and deputy made me lose my place," she explained.

"I don't know where Ms. Lou Ellen is." And she tapped the fingers of her right hand on the counter in front of her.

"I can watch the phones if that's what you need." I had nothing else to do anyway.

Mary considered my offer and then agreed. She showed me

how to fill out a reservation form and how to read the big blue notebook that had most of the answers to the questions people usually asked. She said that she wasn't expecting anyone to check in that morning, so I shouldn't have to worry with that. Then she was gone, saying she'd probably return in twenty minutes.

After she left, the thoughts of names and relations and life and death still churning in my head, I walked over to the table where Lucas had sat earlier and picked up the paper he had been reading. I scanned the front page until I found the article about this man, about Lawrence Franklin. I walked back to the desk behind the counter, sat down, folded the paper, and began to read.

The story was on the bottom of the first page, situated between two pictures. The first one, pasted in the upper left corner, was a recent photograph of the deceased, a posed shot in which he was wearing a shirt and tie and jacket, arms across his chest, a slight smile, and a look that spoke of discomfort or a sense of being ill at ease. Perhaps, I thought, studying his picture, we shared the same dislike for having our photographs taken.

The picture, dated as being from the same year as his death, was a shot from a recent photo directory of the church. It was black and white, but you could see that Mr. Lawrence Franklin was graying a bit, along the edges of his hairline, along the borders of his mustache. He wore glasses, dark frames at least a decade old, and he leaned forward as if the photographer had said words he couldn't hear, as if he was pushing himself to see something more clearly.

The other picture in the paper, farther down on the right side of the story, was a shot of the sandbar where his body had been recovered, a few firemen standing around the edge of the water, a winding piece of tape marking perimeters to keep away reporters and curious bystanders.

There was the ambulance I had seen on the day of the recovery, backed up near the group of people, its door opened wide. The two attendants were standing near the rear of the vehicle. It appeared as if the young woman I recalled seeing had turned and faced the camera just as the shot had been taken, as if she had been surprised by the presence of a photographer and having her picture taken. The man standing with her was staring out over the river. There were shadows cast across the water, an eerie presence looming along the Mississippi.

If you looked at the entire page of the newspaper at once, drawing your vision from left to right, top to bottom, it seemed as if that page had been designed or laid out so that Mr. Franklin appeared to be supervising the event taking place in the second photograph.

The story pasted in the middle of these two photographs told facts and figures of the dead man. It reported that he was born and raised in West Memphis and listed him as a graduate from the local high school and a business college somewhere near Little Rock. It was noted that he had been an award-winning athlete, a runner, and a member of the local Civitan Club, a volunteer at the Boys and Girls Club. It was noted that he was well respected in his community and known for his hard work.

Based upon the short bio of the dead man, he seemed like he

had a good life, a happy life; I wondered again how it was concluded he had committed suicide.

There was a quote from some official person about the fast current in the river, how dangerous the water can be, but there was nothing, it seemed, of what had really occurred in the accident, of the real story.

Mr. Franklin, posed in his business suit, refusing to smile more than he considered necessary, refusing to open his mouth, his eyes, dark and aware—this, I discovered, was the heart of what really happened.

Here were the details of the truth, and they were not reported in the *West Memphis Daily Record*. There was something, I could tell from his photograph, that was not being told.

And just as I was starting to ask a question of myself or to the picture of the dead man, the phone rang. I reached over to answer it.

SIX

Shady Grove Campground," I said, just as Mary had instructed. I searched for a pen and a piece of paper in case there was a message to record.

"Mary?" the voice asked.

"No, this is Rose Franklin," I replied, saying the name with even more confidence than before, claiming it, making it mine. "I'm just helping Mary out."

"Oh."

There was a pause.

"This is Sheriff Montgomery," the voice on the other end said. "From the West Memphis Sheriff's Department."

There was a slight hesitation as if he were waiting for some sign that I understood who he was. I couldn't think of anything friendly to say.

"Tell Mary or Lucas or whoever will be there later today that I'm sending the deputy back out there this afternoon. We got some more questions to ask of the campers, find out if there are any witnesses who might know something about the Franklin death."

I waited.

"It seems Deputy Fisk got run off before he could complete his detail," the sheriff noted.

I smiled, remembering Mary's reaction to the lawman.

"We need to clear some things up before we can close the file on the suicide," he continued.

"Okay," I answered and then asked, "What things?"

"I beg your pardon?" he replied.

"You said you had to clear up some things, what things?"

"Who are you again?" The voice was gruff.

"Rose Franklin," I said.

"You kin to Lawrence?"

"Maybe," I replied, thinking how odd it felt to say such a thing, right and wrong at the same time.

"Well, not that I need to tell you anything," he said sharply, "We just need to check with the rest of the visitors at the campground who were there over the weekend and view a few locations near Shady Grove before we write up the report. I'm trying to understand where the victim got into the river. I think it might have happened near the Boyds' place"—then he stopped as if he realized he was telling more than he needed to.

"It's nothing for you to concern yourself with. And you can tell Mary and Lucas that we can talk to whomever we want. We don't need their permission."

"It's private property," I said. I'm much more assertive on the phone than in person.

"It's police business," he said.

"I'll tell them," I answered. "What time do you think Deputy Fisk will be here?"

And the sheriff hung up.

There are things a woman knows. I don't mean to make it sound like a man wouldn't know the same things, but I can't speak for that part of the human race. I can only speak for my part, the female part. And I don't mean to sound like women know everything all the time. We don't, of course.

I knew my mother was sick before she ever went to the doctor. I was only twelve years old, but I had already acquired that gift of being a woman. I knew it because of the way she touched her chest, lightly, her fingers spread open as if she was trying to contain the clump of multiplying and irregular cells. The way she closed her eyes as if she were praying when she sat down on the sofa after cleaning up the dinner dishes, brief as those moments were, for she would pick up a magazine or look at the mail before you could ask her anything, but it didn't matter; the moments were telling and I was paying attention. And I knew.

I knew she was going to die when I felt the heaviness in the hand of the doctor when he stepped by me, patting me on the head, making his way toward my father. It was just one action, one stupid way an adult acknowledges a child, done to me a million times in my young lifetime, but that time was different and I knew.

I knew she was dead when I awoke at five o'clock in the morning and a bird was sitting on the sill of my bedroom window, perched there like she had been waiting for me to awaken, a sign from God, a tiny bit of pink ribbon in her beak. I lay perfectly still and watched her, a sparrow, small and brown, a mother building a nest, and I knew.

I knew when my brother was leaving home, a month before he turned sixteen. The way he kept avoiding me, locking his door at night, slowly packing things in milk crates and in the trunk of his car, the way he just turned away without yelling when I told him I lost his favorite cassette tape. Even when he lied to Daddy and said he was just going to stay with a friend for the weekend, I knew.

I knew that my father was becoming more and more dangerous and that he drank every night after my mother died. I knew the baby was dead, that my womb was empty, and that my husband didn't mean it when he said he never really wanted children anyway. And I knew that Rip had fallen in love when I saw him sitting across from the girl who looked nothing like me.

I knew I would pass the RN exam, that I would graduate from college, and that I would never be as lovely or as comfortable with pain or as tender as my mother. And once I had seen the photograph of Mr. Franklin, staring over the details of his death, and once I had heard the voice of the sheriff, short and irritated, still needing to find some clue or some answer to a simple suicide, I knew. I knew there was nothing simple about it; I knew it wasn't suicide.

Unfortunately, as I reflected upon my gift of intuition, my

infallible means of knowing, I also reflected upon the fact that even if I knew something was going to happen, even if I could tell the real truth of a situation, I remained paralyzed or ineffective in doing anything about it. There was never a plan made or a series of proactive measures put into place. I was sure that there had always been things that I knew, but even with that knowledge, nothing ever changed.

My mother was sick and soon died. My father drank himself into a stupor. My brother ran away from home. I became a nurse, lost a baby and a husband, became a woman unlike the one I wanted to be. All the things I knew, but could not change. But as I stood in the office of the Shady Grove Campground, convinced that Mr. Franklin had fallen into something more sinister than suicide and that there was something untold about his life and death, I felt a tiny possibility that things could be different this time.

Maybe, I thought, it was just the place, someplace so different from my growing-up place, or maybe it was the time, having left my life. Or maybe, I wondered, standing alone in a campground office, maybe it was me. I was different.

Not just the name. Not just the removal of my husband's infidelity and my father's heavy hand from my identity, giving birth to a new designation. Maybe I was bolder or wiser or less afraid of the things I didn't know and more willing to believe those things I did know.

Maybe I was tired of always being on the outside looking in. Maybe in having packed up my things and left what was behind me, I was ready to be a part of something bigger than myself, ready to be a part of a community, ready to belong. Maybe I was finally tired of being alone, the way I have felt all my life, the way I felt even in my marriage. Perhaps I was finally ready to break through the wall that had been around my heart since the moment my mother died.

It's hard to say why or how, only that it was so. Something was different. I knew.

"Rose Franklin," I said aloud in the empty office. "Rose Franklin is my name and I know that there's more to this story."

"Well, Ms. Rose Franklin, perhaps you can enlighten the rest of us."

The voice surprised me so much that I whipped around, knocking off books and papers from Mary's desk. I hadn't realized there was a back door to the office and that an older woman was now standing directly across from me.

"Good heavens!" I yelled. "Who are you?"

She smiled and held out her hand like a queen. "Rose Franklin, my name is Lou Ellen Johnston Maddox Perkins . . . ," she paused. "Well, there are other last names, but that's more than enough for you to try and remember." She winked.

"I'm from southern Arkansas and I am Rhonda's mother. And I've always known there was more to every story." And she glided over to where I was sitting.

Glided, that's what she did. She didn't just move or walk or get to where it was she was going. Ms. Lou Ellen had been a ballerina, and Ms. Lou Ellen floated, like a feather in midair. She was as smooth as bathwater.

I reached out and touched her fingers. I wasn't sure how to shake such a dainty and royally held hand. Then I started picking up the things that had fallen.

"I'm sorry," I said. "I wasn't expecting anybody else to come by."

She laughed and stepped out of the way giving me more room to gather the fallen papers. "It's quite all right, dear," she said, her words drawn out with a thick Southern accent.

I finished returning things to order and I moved away from the desk and around to the front of the counter, resuming the role of visitor, and giving her the rightful place of the campground manager.

"Mary went to pick up trash," I told her. "I was just watching the office for her."

Ms. Lou Ellen nodded. "Fine," she replied. "I know I'm late. Annie Lester made a run at the pot." She waved her hand across her face. "Swish," she added.

I'm sure I appeared confused.

"Swish, dear. It's a card game."

I shrugged.

"Doesn't matter." And she slid around to the desk and sat down. "You're staying here?" she asked.

I nodded. "Got here yesterday. My car broke down and is being fixed."

"Well, how lovely," she said. "And our Mary has already put you to work?"

I smiled.

"No, I volunteered." Then I added, "I met your daughter and your son-in-law."

"Oh, they've returned?" she asked.

"Yes, but they're not here." I glanced around, thinking how stupid that was to report since the office was clearly empty except for the two of us.

"Yes," she answered. "I'm sure they have things to do at their trailer."

She lifted up the paper I had been reading. "And what story is it that has more to tell?" she asked as she scanned the headlines.

I hesitated. I wasn't sure I wanted to talk about this to anyone. About a minute passed. I was thinking.

She peered at me over the rhinestone reading glasses she was now wearing.

"Lawrence Franklin's suicide," I confessed. "I think there's something else about his death that the police aren't telling."

She raised her eyebrows. "Ah," she replied. "A mystery." She dragged out the syllables of the word *mystery,* making it sound very interesting.

I lowered my eyes.

"Did you talk to Tom?"

And there it was again. That flutter in my chest.

"No, but Mary has told me about him."

"Tom knows almost every mystery of this community and he loves to talk about that river."

I nodded.

She folded the paper and looked at me. "Besides, he and the dead man grew up together. They were good friends," she added quietly, confirming what Mary had already told me. "He can an-swer any question you might have."

Mary rushed in about this time. She was huffing. Her long hair was twisted in a bun on top of her head, but large pieces were falling down. Her face was red, flushed from her work and her hurry.

"You finally here?" she said to Ms. Lou Ellen.

"Yes, dear," she responded. "And now so are you."

Then she turned in my direction. "And how lovely to have made the acquaintance of Ms. Rose Franklin."

Mary looked at me. "Thank you, Rose. Any call?"

I shook my head at first. Then I remembered the sheriff. "Oh, the policeman is coming back out here today."

Mary rolled her eyes.

"Something about checking out possible locations where the dead man entered the river and he intends to speak to the other campers."

I stepped toward the door. "It's about the suicide," I added.

"The one you expect that there's more to tell about," Ms. Lou Ellen said in that dramatic way she had said the word *mystery* previously.

I nodded slowly, smiled.

"Well, then you better get busy because the sheriff likes things at the river very tidy." She slid off her glasses and they hung around her neck on a gold chain.

"He'll be here every day if he thinks somebody knows more of the story than he does."

"Aahhh," Mary said in exasperation, moving behind the

counter. She untied her hair and it fell down across her shoulders. "Sheriff just mad at Lucas for not selling."

"Well, there is that," Ms. Lou Ellen added.

"What was Lucas not selling?" I asked, standing at the door.

"The property, darling." Ms. Lou Ellen handed Mary a mirror, but she just shook her head at her and started twisting and smoothing down her hair.

"The campground?" I asked.

"Yes, Shady Grove Campground." The older woman returned the mirror to the front drawer of the desk.

"I thought it was some developer from Tennessee who tried to buy this land." I remembered the trucker mentioning it on the day I arrived.

"The sheriff's brother from Nashville," Mary answered. "He the one wanting to buy it. Sheriff was a big investor."

"Seems like this would be the perfect spot for a rich man's river dwelling," Ms. Lou Ellen said with a smile. "Some people just don't like the idea of a campground in their proximity. And some people particularly don't like that this campground is owned by Lucas and Rhonda."

Then she leaned back in her chair, stretching her hands across her lap, studying her nails. "Too many strangers coming and going," she added.

"Sheriff been here causing trouble ever since Lucas say no." Mary tightened the pull on her hair, flipping it and twisting it into a bun, then tying it up using a pencil from the counter.

"How long ago was that?" I asked.

"Six months, maybe seven, I'd say, wouldn't you, Mary?" Ms. Lou Ellen asked.

"Almost a year," she answered. "Doesn't matter. Can't find nothing here."

She smoothed the sides of her hair. "No sign of drugs, gambling, no crime at Shady Grove."

"That's right, dear," Ms. Lou Ellen said. "We're as clean as old bones bleached in the sun."

Ms. Lou Ellen, I am learning, has a very dramatic way of holding a conversation. She's full of lines like this one.

"'Old bones bleached in the sun,'" I repeated. "I guess that's pretty clean." And even though I didn't speak of it at the time, I wondered if the campground and Ms. Lou Ellen's daughter and son-in-law were really as spotless as she believed.

"Yes, dear, very clean indeed," she replied.

"Well," I said as a means of departure. "It's getting late and I'm hungry again. I think I'll go fix myself a sandwich."

Mary glanced up at the clock on the wall. "The day almost half over," she said and shook her head as if she was behind on her daily tasks. "Thank you for watching the office."

She returned the blue book to the top drawer, placed a couple of pens in the cup on the top shelf.

"Perhaps we should reduce her rate of stay since she performed a bit of my work today." Ms. Lou Ellen winked at me and waited for Mary to respond.

"Nah, that's fine." I said, figuring Rip would pay the bill anyway. "I was glad to help out."

"It was a pleasure meeting you, Ms. Lou Ellen," I said.

"The pleasure was all mine." She drew every word out, punching each syllable like a poet.

"Well, good-bye then," I said to them both.

"Bye, dear," Ms. Lou Ellen said.

Mary threw up her hand at me while she continued arranging and rearranging the items on the counter.

I waved my good-bye and walked out of the office, making my way to the river.

SEVEN

I fell in love at 11:59 A.M. on a Tuesday, a hot June day when the sun stood alone in the clear blue Arkansas sky. Just before the falling, there were highway sounds off in the distance, jake brakes on eighteen-wheelers slowing down as they headed toward the construction work on Highway 55, southbound. There were river sounds, water slapping against the sides of a two-tiered tug and barge going toward Memphis against the muddy current, waterfowl—sandpipers, I think—splashing themselves along the edge of the smallest pond.

There was a gentle hum of a conversation between two men, fishing talk, lines and lures and catches. A light breeze blew through the leaves on the small, knotty birch trees that lined the bank. A swishing sound, like something going by too fast. A car on gravel near the office. A woman speaking softly to her dog. A train whistle, far away, but moving in the direction of the railroad crossing at First Street and Broadway.

I was forty-one years old, single, recently divorced, not looking for companionship. I had my grandmother Burns's narrow
chin, my mother's dark eyes and thick hair, her father's peach
skin, fifteen extra pounds, and I was on my way to somewhere
other than where I was. I was walking, not too fast, not thinking
that I was paying close attention to the path or the sky or the
sounds of the late morning. I was thinking about what I had to
eat in the refrigerator of my camper.

I fell in love with Thomas Sawyer as soon as I laid my eyes
on him, maybe before, since I recognized him when I saw him,
knew I had waited for him for more years than I had been
married.

Dark as a thundercloud, tall, lean-boned, looking ten years
younger than what he was; I felt him before I saw him. I sped up
my pace without even understanding why, just to get closer to
him. Knew I loved him even before he stood up, turned around,
and faced me.

It was the way I had always hoped falling in love would be.

"You're new," was what he said to me, even though he doesn't
remember those being his first words.

He says that he said to me, "Well, here you are." And even if
that wasn't what he said it would make for a more interesting
story, but that isn't what he said. He said, "You're new."

He was standing up from the chair that he had placed near
the short pier at the big pond. There was a bucket hidden in the
tall grass. He gently laid his fishing pole beside where he sat, and
was getting ready to reach into the small cooler he had next to

him, going to get a soda and the egg salad sandwich he had made and packed for his lunch.

I was heading the long way to river row, to my camper, going past the big pond, on the other side of the office. So unusually attuned to the things around me, all the sounds and the signs that something important was about to take place, I almost walked right into him.

"New?" I asked, surprised at the observation, stunned at the level of emotion filling me on such a clear and satisfied morning, dizzy-headed from the way things were spinning, outside in the white sun and inside the tight spaces of my heart.

"New," he said again.

I think my mouth stood wide-open.

"At Shady Grove." And he smiled.

"Yes," I answered, pulling my mouth shut, pressing my lips together. "Yes, that's right."

"I thought I saw Ledford drop you off yesterday."

He's been watching me, I thought. Without either one of us knowing it, he's been waiting for me like I've been waiting for him.

My first love, Rip, my ex-husband, was not waiting for me when we met. Rip has never waited for anybody. I just came across his path when he was getting ready to graduate from college, and he didn't have a job or a place to live or a plan for what he wanted. Marrying a nurse, a young woman settled and submissive, buying a house near his parents; I was just a means to make sense of the complexities of life to a boy needing direction.

Oh, I don't want to sound completely pessimistic about my marriage. I do think Rip loved me, wanted to make a life with me. I just think I could have been any girl, that anybody would have been qualified for the position he was seeking to fill. I just happened to be the one who walked through the door when he opened it. I just happened to be the one he met on the night he had decided he needed something stable to which to cling.

And at the age of nineteen, almost finished with nursing school, already living on my own and paying my bills, I was the poster child for stability.

And Rip was a good-looking boy. He was every girl's idea of a great catch. I thought of nothing except how lucky I was that he chose me. It never crossed my mind that it might not be a choice that lasted very long. Nor did I think that the choice for a wife is altogether different from the choice for a woman to love. Unfortunately, it took me more than twenty years to figure that out.

Tom wasn't looking for stability when we met. He wasn't looking for an anchor or a stronghold or a port to dock his boat. He wasn't looking for anything. He was just waiting. He says now that the not-looking was what made our love so sweet to him in the beginning.

He says that it's the surprise of love that gives the relationship its strength. That it's not the attraction or the devotion or even the commitment. It's the surprise, he says, the unexpectedness of finding somebody that fits you, the unlikelihood, especially at a late date, of finding another complete human being

DOWN BY THE RIVERSIDE

who matches up to you eyeball to eyeball and who loves you the way you've always longed to be loved.

That, he says, is the best thing about living and the most important gift of life. The surprise of finding love at exactly the moment you're not looking.

"Rose," I said to him before he asked.

"I'm Rose. Rose Franklin Burns Griffith. Rose Franklin."

I wanted no detail of my life withheld from this man fishing on the Tuesday I fell in love.

"That's a powerful string of names," he replied and then said, "Thomas Sawyer."

He wiped his fingers on a red handkerchief that was stuck in his front shirt pocket, then reached out to shake my hand.

"Tom," I replied. "Tom Sawyer," I repeated, our hands still clasped. "I've heard of you."

He pulled his hand away gently and nodded his head slowly. "Yep," he said. "It's a common name."

"No," I replied, realizing he thought I was making fun of him.

"No," I said again. "Not that way." I was embarrassed. "Well, I mean, I have heard of that name, too. But that's not what I mean," I stammered. "Mary and Ms. Lou Ellen said I should talk to you."

He lifted his eyebrows, interested. He studied my face, which I felt start to flush.

"About what?" he asked and I wasn't sure what he meant.

I paused, then shook my head, demonstrating my confusion.

"Mary and Ms. Lou Ellen said that you should talk to me about what?" he asked.

"Oh, right," I said, suddenly remembering.

"Uh . . ." I stumbled with my words, "About the river and this area." I glanced around. "About Lawrence Franklin."

His head jerked up when I said his name.

"You were friends, right?" I asked, hoping I wasn't being too nosy.

He walked down a couple of steps to the bank and pulled his line out of the water. He stuck the pole in the ground beside the bucket, the line swinging around the top, and he sat down on the pier across from where I was standing. I loomed over him.

He peered up at me, the sun causing him to squint, smoothed his hands across the tops of his legs, and said, "Have a seat." He motioned with his hand to his folding canvas chair.

I sat down.

He asked, "So what do you want to know?"

I paused, thinking about the unformed questions, about the things Mary and Ms. Lou Ellen thought I should ask, about his relationship with the dead man, about life on the Mississippi.

"Tell me something about your friend," I replied.

He glanced away for a second and then turned and faced the water. I could tell that he was thinking about what he wanted to say.

He cleared his throat.

"Lawrence loved this place. Except for the time we were both away at war or at school, we fished together at this very spot practically once a week for more than forty years." He nodded slowly as if he was remembering each and every time.

"We grew up together. Our lives were very similar," he added.

I didn't comment. I figured he wasn't waiting for anything I could say in reply.

"And we were both drawn to this river. It's as if her stories bound us together and bound us to her banks. She was our primary teacher in life."

I considered what he was saying, thought about the relationship the two men had with each other and with the Mississippi River.

"What stories?" I asked.

"Lots of them," he answered.

He paused and could see I was waiting for one or two that he might share, and he decided to oblige.

He smiled. "The Mississippi," he said proudly, each syllable a dance across his tongue. "Well, let's see. The Indians were here first, of course. The Chicasaws. The first white man who discovered it was a Spanish explorer named de Soto in 1542. He wrote others about it, but they must not have been very interested in it because nobody else came for more than a hundred years.

"Then later a man by the name of La Salle returned to the area. He sailed it and wrote about it, but again it was awhile before anybody else from Europe wanted to visit this part of the new country."

He scratched his chin and continued. He apparently enjoyed giving history lessons to newcomers.

"In 1863 the basin was known as the 'Body of the Nation.' It was said that it would contain Spain five times, France six times, and Italy ten times. According to Mr. Mark Twain in 1883, if you consider the Missouri River its main branch, the Mississippi is the longest river in the world, but we now consider both the Amazon and the Nile as being longer. Every year the river shortens by thirty to fifty miles, but today we estimate it as being about 2,350 miles long.

"Twain also claimed that it was the crookedest, and I guess that idea has not been challenged. Every year it deposits millions of tons of mud into the Gulf of Mexico. And because of this, it has also been called 'the Great Sewer.'"

Then Tom leaned forward.

"That's just the details though," he noted. "Not a real story. Maybe you'd be most interested in the story about the buried treasure."

"Sure," I answered. "What story is that?"

"The story of the slave's gold," he answered.

Then he blew out a breath as if he was thinking of the best way to begin, as if it was the kind of story he both liked and disliked.

I settled in his chair, forgetting that I was hungry or sitting in the sun without sunblock. I was thinking that it was about the oddest thing in my life to be lounging at a pond with the man I was going to love, listening to him tell me about life on the Mississippi River. Odd maybe, but I was so caught up in what he was saying, I was sitting on the edge of that canvas fold-up seat.

"In 1855, a few years before the start of the war, a slave by the name of Percy Dalton escaped from a sugarcane plantation in

Hardwood, Louisiana. He hadn't planned on running, hadn't considered how he would do it or where he would go, but one night there was a thunderstorm and lightning caused a fire at the stables and the place went crazy just long enough so that he found himself with the perfect opportunity to steal a horse and start riding toward the river. He knew it would be hours before anyone missed him because of the fire and the storm and the dark night and the frenzy of disaster.

"He was new to Hardwood, having only recently been sold from a plantation in Mississippi, not too far from his new quarters, but far enough never to be able to see his wife or be a father to their two children."

Tom stopped, stood up, came very near to me, reached into the cooler and took out his soda. He popped the top, poured part of it in an empty water bottle that he had and handed the can to me. I took it and thanked him. We drank a few swallows and he told more of the story.

"When Percy ran, he thought about trying to get to his wife and children, but he knew the chances that he could find them and help them escape were very slim. So he decided instead that he would make his way north, earn some money, then send somebody back to the South to purchase his family.

"Percy Dalton rode the stolen horse from Hardwood up to Laurel Hill and across the state border. He rode hard through the forest along the banks of the river to what is now Saint Joseph, where the horse finally died from exhaustion and the sun started rising on them both. Percy buried the horse and hid there, near the lakes, fighting moccasins for clean water and a black bear for food. Finally, six days later, he met a Quaker minister by the name of Eugene Carter who helped him find freedom. They rafted and hid all the way up the river through Mississippi then Arkansas, through Tennessee and up to Illinois, the first free state they came to."

Tom took another swallow. I did as well. Then he reached into the cooler again and took out his sandwich, giving me half. I took that, too.

"He worked in a slaughterhouse for about a year, learned how to read and write, found a way to pass notes and messages back to his family in Mississippi, telling them where he was and what he was doing. Then he met up with some men from Georgia who were looking for a crew of miners to go out west. They had heard about an area near the confluence of Cherry Creek and the South Platte River, in Denver, Colorado, and that there were deposits of very pure gold there.

"This was sometime late summer of 1857 and this group of prospectors didn't care about where a man came from or about race or history. They just wanted strong backs and tight lips. So, Percy went along and worked for two years. He earned and saved enough money, he thought, to buy his wife, their ten-year-old son, and an eight-year-old daughter."

Tom took a bite of his sandwich and seemed to enjoy my intense interest in his storytelling. He didn't take long before he started up again.

"Now in July of 1860, a banking firm from Leavenworth, Kansas, by the name of Clark, Gruber, and Company decided to establish a mint in this new gold mining area and issue gold coins. You see," Tom said, enjoying the history lesson, "as more and more people went west and the major gold strikes heated up, the population in these western towns grew and commerce quickly started to feel the need for more money. So this banking firm bought machinery and equipment in New York and Philadelphia, got it to Colorado, and began producing coins that actually contained more gold than the coins minted by the government.

"This," Tom said with flavor, "is the means of payment that Percy Dalton received for his work. He had about one thousand dollars in these gold coins. And with that money and a heart longing for his beloved family, he walked all the way to Illinois, found Friend Eugene, and asked him if he would do the buying of his wife, Lavender, and their children, Percy, Jr., and Lydia. And after not too much deliberation, the gentle abolitionist agreed. The Quaker minister set out on a steamboat from Cairo, Illinois, in September of 1860 headed for Vicksburg, Mississippi, where Percy's family lived.

"Only a few months before the start of the war, things were unsettled along the river and the steamboat had a hard time returning to the South. It was stopped by the militia, ran into a violent thunderstorm, and was attacked at least twice, but the preacher wrote to Percy that the money that he carried was still secure. He said they were planning to stop the next day in Memphis to buy supplies and fix a broken section of the vessel and that he would write again from there."

Tom took a deep breath. "Percy never heard from the Quaker again."

We both took bites out of our sandwiches. In the pause between us, I wondered about a steamboat heading down the
river. I watched the muddy current and thought about folks living on these banks almost 150 years ago.

"They never found out what happened?" I asked, curious
about all these people I had just learned about.

"Percy risked everything and came down himself. He had
some papers made up to show that he was free, but still, it was a
mighty foolish thing for a black man to do in that time." Tom
shook his head.

"War about to start. Tempers flaring. Him a runaway. The
river so dangerous." He took another bite. "But that's the crazy
thing about love." He looked at me.

I blushed.

There was a pause.

"So, what happened?"

"Well, there was a big storm that blew through while the
Quaker was supposed to have been here. Floodwaters rose
about forty feet, put everything within six miles underwater.
Lots of people died, lost everything. The steamboat was hit
pretty hard, capsized. Not much left to sort through. Everybody
just speculated the minister, like some of the others on board,
drowned, and that the money like everybody else's wealth and
personal possessions, was lost in the river."

Tom finished the sandwich and brushed the crumbs off of
his mouth.

"Percy got here after the floods had subsided, but there was nothing to be found. They said the steamboat captain had gone, that there were no survivors left in town. Nobody knew anything about the minister or the money, and finally as the war began and the river traffic was being halted, I guess Percy returned to Cairo and then to Denver."

"Without his wife?" I asked.

"Without anything," Tom replied.

I waited out of respect for a dead man's hardship.

"So, what's the story now? Why is this such an interesting tale for people in West Memphis?"

Tom took a drink, smiled slightly as if I had discovered his secret.

"Ah, you were paying attention."

I smiled back.

"Some folks say the gold is here. That the Quaker came across the river from Memphis and hid it over here before he was killed or swept away. There are some people who believe he knew the storm was coming and he put it away for safekeeping."

I nodded. "So everybody's looking for this gold?"

"This gold is pretty valuable today. Clark, Gruber, and Company, along with several other minting operations, shut down in a couple of years. In 1863, Clark's company sold their outfit to the United States government and thereby no longer made these particular coins. So, you can see that these coins are quite rare. There are some of them where only five or ten are known to exist. For anybody to find this bag of gold, fame and fortune would be their reward."

"This is a good story," I said, thinking about all the folks who love a good treasure search, love the thought of finding gold, of making history.

Then I thought again about Percy and his family, what the coins meant to him, how much they took from his life. "Whatever happened to Lavender and the children?" I asked.

Tom shook his head. "That part nobody knows," he answered. "I guess like so many slaves at that time, they were killed. Once Percy returned to Denver the war started and there were no more letters from him found. As far as anybody knows Percy and Lavender never saw each other again."

We were both silent for a while. I thought about the brokenness of a man and a woman, the plight of aborted love. I stretched my eyes and thoughts across the Mississippi River, the dark body of moving, living water that gave one slave his freedom, only to steal it away in the end.

I thought about the woman, Lavender, the way she must have watched every day for the coming of a stranger who would bring back the night stars that had been hidden from her since Percy was sold, the music at dawn that she lost when he never returned from the cane field, some man who would give to her once again the only thing good about her living.

I thought about how long she must have watched the skies and the winding roads, how long she kept her few things packed, her children ready to go, how desperately she clung to hope. I wondered when she gave up, if she ever did, and what became of a woman with too much grief.

I considered this Quaker, this man who was connected to

Percy and who risked his own life to help him escape. I thought about his soul, if he knew he was in great peril and what his final prayer on this earth would have been; I wondered, though he had proven himself in rafting to Cairo with Percy, if he had been smart enough to estimate the damage of an arriving storm and knew a safe place to hide a bag of gold coins. So many questions, I thought, so much life and death and dreams and plans buried in the dark mud of a river.

Then suddenly while I was thinking about the minister's death, about what might have happened to him, I remembered Lawrence Franklin; I wondered if these two stories were somehow related.

"Was your friend Lawrence interested in the buried treasure?" I asked, watching for his response.

He shook his head and gave a little laugh.

"Nah," he answered. "He found it to be a nice story, but he had no concern for finding gold. Lawrence was never one very interested in having a lot of money."

I waited.

"He was only interested in giving rest to lost souls."

He could see I was not following his explanation.

"Lawrence focused mostly on another story of tragedy. He believed there had been a place somewhere along the banks where folks had been buried and he wanted to buy and dedicate part of this area to be a cemetery for folks who had nowhere else to go, folks who died homeless. He wanted to know who each one was and honor them with markers."

I nodded.

I knew the deceased had been a funeral director; Ledford had told me. "Were they slaves?" I asked.

Thomas nodded. "Yes, but Lawrence wasn't particular about whom he served. He just hated the idea of all of the loose spirits floating around the river."

I considered all of the heartache and sorrow that floated on the surface, all of the longings and losses swirling in the currents below.

"There are lots of stories of afflicted folks who met their deaths here—" He stopped.

I knew he was thinking about Lawrence, his friend, a man who died in the very place he loved, the place so full of memories and trouble.

I paused for a minute, watching a fishing boat move across the river.

"I met a deacon from Mr. Franklin's church a little while ago in the office," I reported.

"He didn't believe your friend had committed suicide. He didn't think he would do such a thing."

Tom didn't reply. I could see that he was thinking about his friend, thinking about what had been said about him.

I was just getting ready to ask Tom about what he thought of the stories that were circulating that Lawrence Franklin had committed suicide when I heard a vehicle pull up behind us.

I turned around in my seat and saw that it was a police car. True to the sheriff's words, Deputy Fisk had returned.

EIGHT

Mr. Sawyer," the deputy said as he got out of the car. His uniform was still crisp, his black shoes shined. He placed his hat under his arm as he stepped in our direction, and I noticed that he had just gotten a haircut. It was very short on both the top and the sides. A crew cut; he now looked severe.

Tom nodded and I wondered how the two men knew each other, if they were friends or if it had more to do with the deputy's earlier statement about the "history" at Shady Grove.

The officer walked over to me since I was closest to the car.

"Ms. Franklin," he said, surprising me that he remembered my name.

"Deputy," I said in response.

"Going to be warm today," he said to both of us as he wiped his brow with the back of his hand and then placed his hat squarely on his head. He was staring out toward the pond behind Tom, seemed to be taking inventory of the things he might not have seen earlier in the day.

"It'll rain this evening," Tom answered, without standing up. There was no respect given to the young officer.

I remained in my seat as well. Deputy Fisk seemed uncomfortable standing over us and he shifted his weight from side to side.

"Nice storm last night," he said as a means to keep up a conversation. He had his sunglasses on and they added to his authority.

Tom nodded.

"River's still high," he said, a continued effort in making small talk.

"Yep," Tom responded. Then it went quiet for a while.

"You here about Mr. Franklin again," I said this to let him know that it was fine to go ahead and conduct his business. Having just discovered each other and the genuine possibility of love, neither Tom nor myself seemed very interested in carrying on a polite discourse with the man.

He made a deep exhaling noise, a snort, as if it humored him that I was naming his affairs.

"Yes, the sheriff has a few more questions." Then he sighed as if maybe he shouldn't say anything else, but then he thought better of it.

"Frankly, it seems like a waste of my time, but I'm just doing what I'm told."

Tom didn't say a word. He dropped his chin in his hand, paying close attention to the uniformed officer.

"So, who are the questions for?" I asked.

"Just the folks who were here last weekend."

I nodded and faced Tom. He was watching me. I liked the feel of his eyes on me.

"Well, that doesn't include myself, so I guess I'm excused from the midday interrogation."

I put down the can of soda next to the chair. I had drunk all of what was there and was feeling a little thirsty. I remembered that I had a big pitcher of tea in my camper and I started thinking how good that would taste.

The policeman laughed quietly to himself. Then he rested his hands on the items attached to his belt, his gun and nightstick. He spread his legs a bit, held out his chest. He was like a bird showing off new feathers.

"What about you, Mr. Sawyer?" he asked, acting more informal, but still calling Tom Mr. Sawyer.

"You and the victim were known to be good friends, what do you think about this suicide?"

I waited to see how Tom would respond, if he received the invitation to deliver an opinion as a friendly one or if he looked at it as I had, as a manner of tactical maneuvering.

He didn't say anything at first. Then he took a deep breath, staring out over the river behind the policeman, behind me. I could see how he measured the words. I could see how the question bothered him.

"What do I think?" He paused, giving the question deep consideration.

A breeze lifted our moods just for a moment.

"I think the sheriff seems awfully interested in the death of a black man."

His honesty and candor surprised me. I smiled. I liked it. And the simplicity of it, the tidiness did ring true.

The young policeman didn't change positions. It was clear he was listening.

Tom continued, "Seems like he's more interested in Lawrence that he was in Mabel Kennedy's daughter when she left home to go to work on a Tuesday morning and then went missing a couple of years ago."

He stared at the deputy. "You-all ever figure out what happened to her?"

The deputy didn't respond.

"He seems more interested in Lawrence's death than he was when Jack Valentine's body washed up summer before last—" He stopped.

"How about that one? You find out what happened in that case?"

The deputy just turned and looked away.

"Nah, I didn't think so. See, both of those victims were people of color and both received a less-than-adequate investigation, if you ask me."

The deputy folded his arms across his chest.

"So, here's what I think," and I could tell he was using more words with this young officer than he usually did with the law, demonstrating a bit of generosity.

"Sheriff Montgomery must have an insurance policy on

Lawrence Franklin, otherwise he wouldn't be sending you down here twice in one day, searching for clues about a black man who everybody thinks killed himself."

Then he waited again. "That's what I think."

Deputy Fisk was red-faced now, but I don't think it was anger or embarrassment for what Tom said. I just think he was real hot. He was wearing a lot of clothes and the temperature had risen since the late morning had now become early afternoon.

He relaxed a bit, dropped his hands to his sides. "You two were working together on something out here, weren't you?"

The deputy apparently wasn't going to let Tom's speech on injustice stop his questioning.

Tom shook his head as if he couldn't believe the deputy was asking him the question.

"The sheriff knew what Lawrence was doing out here. Montgomery knew he was looking for the burial site of those dead people off that slave boat. Lawrence was trying to get everybody he knew to help him locate those bodies. So, yeah, like a lot of folks, I was helping him." He blew out a breath.

"So, to answer your question, yes, Lawrence and I were working together, trying to find out where the old burial ground was and trying to figure out how we could bury the dead properly—" He stopped.

"There a crime in that?" he asked.

The deputy shook his head. "Nope, never meant to say there was," he answered. "I'm just doing my job," he added.

"You know if he ever found it?" he asked, watching Tom closely.

Tom just shrugged his shoulders. It was easy to see that he was through answering the policeman's questions.

Then Deputy Fisk turned to me. I felt him waiting for something.

"You got any new ideas?"

"Me?" I was surprised by his question. I knew I didn't have stories from West Memphis. Nobody knew who I was. And even if I had formed an opinion about the death of Mr. Franklin in the few hours since I last saw the policeman, I certainly didn't expect him to ask me about it.

"Why would I have any thoughts about this?" I asked, twisting myself in the chair so that I was staring into the young man's face, trying to see if I recognized him from the time I was down on the banks when they brought the body in. I studied him, but I just couldn't recall seeing him before he came to my door earlier that day.

"Sheriff said that you told him that you may in fact be related to Mr. Franklin. He seems to think maybe your showing up in West Memphis on the day we found the dead man's body might be more than a coincidence."

I could feel him watching me, the same way my father would study me when he thought I was lying about something, when he assumed he had caught me in deceit. And suddenly, my mind was made up. I didn't like the young man. I didn't like his shiny black shoes or his freshly starched uniform. I didn't like his short haircut or his police-issued dark sunglasses.

I didn't like his disrupting my falling in love or the way he was following orders from a man who obviously had some personal agenda with Mr. Lawrence Franklin. And I especially didn't like the permission he gave himself to ask strangers, ask me, for personal information. I was no longer comfortable with him standing over me, judging me.

"Well," I answered, "whether or not it is only coincidence that I'm in West Memphis at this particular time is a larger issue than I'm prepared to discuss. I believe that life is full of events that bear meaning and consequence that we don't ever fully comprehend." It must have been the new love lending me the confidence to talk like I was talking.

"I can tell you that I was driving on Interstate Forty, westbound. My car broke down. It's at Jimmy Novack's. I'm staying at Shady Grove because this is where Ledford Pickering dropped me off yesterday afternoon."

Each of my words was clearly enunciated. It was the way I learned to address my father's questions, the way I learned how to respond to perceived hostile inquiries.

"And all of these facts can be substantiated by the mechanic, the trucker, and the office personnel." I ended my answer with a forceful nod of my head. A period. An exclamation point. I was finished. I had said everything I was going to say.

The change in my voice, its slightly raised tone, the defensive quality, were immediately registered by both Tom and the deputy; they appeared somewhat startled at my response.

And after I said it, as good as it felt in the delivery, I was embarrassed of my sensitivities, left more vulnerable by my reaction than I would have been if I had just answered the man's question.

It's true what the psychology experts say. Years into adulthood, the unhealed scars of a child still pucker and bleed with the slightest touch. I still surprise myself with how quickly I draw blood.

Tom raised an eyebrow, leaned back a little on his arms.

"Coincidence." The deputy nodded when he said it, making it clear that I knew he had heard me. "This has been noted."

I turned back around in the chair, facing Tom. He winked at me and it settled me, grounded me, covered over my displeasure, and I gave deep consideration to the possibility that nothing about this visit or place or relationship had anything to do with coincidence.

Deputy Fisk noticed the exchange, nodded his head again, and folded his arms across his chest.

"Okay," he said. It was his way of taking leave.

"I'm going to go around and talk to the guy in the cabin, the young couple on the other end of the row, and that family from Kentucky. They're the only folks who were camped by the river who are still here."

After having just unloaded on him like I did, I had not expected that he would be telling us his plans, but I guess he was just reciting it for himself, a way of naming his tasks. I recognized the behavior because I had done the same thing when I had a full day at the hospital.

And, of course, I knew that the family from Kentucky was Clara and her sister and parents; I considered informing him that they were at the hospital and weren't in their camper. But I just decided that I had said enough and to let him discover their departure on his own.

He cleared his throat, acting as if he wasn't sure how to exit our company. "Thank you for your help," he finally said to both of us. "Ya'll enjoy the afternoon."

"Anytime," Tom answered. Though I doubt that he really meant that.

I just smiled and said nothing. The policeman got into his car and drove to the sites behind me. I heard his car pull out of the gravel onto the dirt road.

Tom waited before saying anything about my conversation with the policeman. I glanced away from him and was trying to think of how I should explain my relationship with my father, how to say what I felt about police officers, my history, my opinions; I searched the river for clues.

After a few minutes of silence, I turned back and saw that look of pure sweetness on his face, and I realized he wasn't going to ask me a thing.

He was just going to let what I said rise up on the wind and disappear. And I realized that part of why I was being drawn to Shady Grove Campground was not just the easy breeze on the river or the slow way the day unfolds, I was also finding myself attached to this spot on the Mississippi because I was learning that like the prayers of Lucas, Rhonda, and Mary, not everything has to be spoken out loud.

"You want something else to eat?" Tom asked.

I nodded. The half of the sandwich had not filled me up.

"I got peanut butter crackers at my camper. Iced tea," I answered.

He grinned at me. "Food and wine of the gods," he responded.

We gathered up his things, set the chair and cooler next to the cane pole and the old white bucket at the pier, and walked together to site number Seventy-six, to my travel trailer—away from the office and the pond and Deputy Fisk—right at the edge of the river.

He waited while I went inside and brought out the food. I watched from the window as he wiped off the table and the benches.

I put everything in a plastic bag and headed to where he sat and joined him.

When I noticed the time on my watch, it was after one o'clock in the afternoon and I realized I had been in love for more than one hour. Upon reflection, I do believe it was the finest hour of my existence up to that exact moment in life. But at the time, I understood I was neither able to explain it or define it, I only knew that I was so full of pleasure and joy and complete satisfaction in that brilliant summer day, that there was nothing nor anybody who could tamper with or destroy the delighted nature of my heart.

We ate peanut butter crackers and drank glasses of cold tea. We sat at the picnic table down by the river and had no cause to speak of death or life or even beauty. It was all stretched out before us.

The afternoon, like the Mississippi, sped past.

NINE

When Clara and her mother returned from the hospital in Memphis, the weariness draped across their shoulders like old wool scarves. Deputy Fisk had left, and Tom and I had shared a pitcher of tea and a list of our favorite things.

We named flavors of ice cream—chocolate for me, butter pecan for him—singers—he claimed Ray Charles, I picked Patsy Cline—and our favorite place to visit—both choosing the ocean and the time of day, again in agreement, saying that it depends completely upon the day.

We had spoken of our childhood dreams, where we had learned our greatest lessons, his from war, mine from love, and the grief we both felt in the loss of a parent. His father, my mother, and how we both thought of them, every single morning in the first hour of our waking.

He told me how he studied engineering at Memphis State

University, but left school his junior year to sign up for military service because he was convinced that his father still needed a reason to be proud of his son, how he was one of the last men in the Navy to enter the Vietnam War and that he was there for only six months when they ended missions and ordered his ship stateside.

He explained that just two months before he returned to West Memphis, his father died, and that he was never able to show him the two Purple Heart medals he won when he shattered his knee and ankle after a bomb exploded on the road where he was driving his commanding officer from the ship to a remote base on land. He was never able to place in his father's hands the Bronze and Silver Stars he was awarded for pulling the officer out of the burning jeep, nor could he show him the letter of special commendation he was given for the design work he did on underwater listening devices that the Navy still uses.

He said that he came back from Vietnam uninterested in science or engineering, uninterested in finishing college or building things, that the only thing which he still felt pleasure for was history. So he bought a trailer using the money he had saved during the summers of his teenaged years, leased a lot on the other side of the quarry that was next to Shady Grove, and read everything he could find about the South, about war, about Africa, and about the Mississippi River.

He started work at the docks on the other side of the river, the Tennessee side, he said. He worked for a long time, but then his knee hurt so often and so acutely that he took an early retirement and lived off his disability.

I told him about being a nurse, how fulfilling I found it to know things about the human body, how I was fascinated with the way things work, how I loved the heart and how consistently it pumped, in good times and bad.

We talked about Shady Grove, the fine location of the campground on the banks of the river, the hard edges to both Lucas and Rhonda, and how I felt both drawn to them and afraid of them at the same time, how Mary, in her tedious and high-strung way, held the place together. We talked about the recent arrival of the police, and even though he never asked, I told him about my father and the long hard way I grew up.

We spoke of summer fruits, peaches and berries, and the best way to make a cobbler crust—biscuit, not pie dough, Arkansas politics, the ease of interstate driving, the way his knee still ached on rainy days, and how we both, though neither of us had too much experience, preferred travel by train.

Finally, in conclusion of talk about shipping methods and river commerce, I asked him what had been on my mind earlier, the things I wanted to know that had been prompted by his treasure story, the gold at the river.

I asked him to tell me what he knew about Lawrence Franklin.

He said that in West Memphis, and particularly on the south side, it was a tight-knit community. Everybody knew everybody. He said that he and Lawrence grew up together, were childhood playmates, ran track together, went on double dates together, but that the years and the family business, college, military service, pulled them apart.

As adults, he said, as men who fished together, shared dreams together, he thought that they were good friends, but that the older he got the less sure he became that he really knew someone anyway.

I thought then about Rip, all the years we lived together, the evening meals when we sorted through the events of the day, the mornings when we dreamed, all the times I thought we were unfolding in front of each other, all the things I thought we were and yet learned later, we were not.

"Lawrence," Tom said after I asked him what kind of man he was, "did not want to be an undertaker at first. It was handed to him, like the history of this place or the spelling of his last name. He had no choice since his father trained him from a child, his grandfather, too. Even as a boy, he dreaded what he knew his grown-up years would entail."

"But he did it anyway?" I asked, already knowing the answer.

"It's a hard thing telling a father no."

And I knew right then that even if there was nothing else, Lawrence and I were bound by the same household burden.

"So you think he was depressed then? That it was suicide?"

Tom shrugged his shoulders. And that was when I heard a car pull up. I turned to see the van drive forward and park at the trailer beside mine.

"No," he answered. "But I doubt we'll ever know the truth." He added, "The law of the land doesn't have a very good history of delivering justice for minorities."

He paused a minute and turned to a more personal part of the relationship and the death.

"But maybe it was suicide, I don't know. Lawrence wasn't ever much of a talker and never really a person who expressed great emotion, but I do think he was content with his life. Once he took over for his father, he had great respect for the business; he took it as some kind of calling. And I know he was excited about finding this burial ground, that he had real purpose in trying to locate it and get it designated as a historical site. That was my job," he noted. "I was trying to figure out how one goes about getting that designation. It's a lot more complicated than you think."

I nodded.

The mother got out of the driver's side. Clara was riding beside her. I noticed the father and Jolie were not with them.

"But it's true, isn't it?" Tom asked quietly. "You never really know about folks, what they're hiding, what pulls at them, what it is that makes them get out of bed in the morning or the thing that finally pushes them to jump in a river."

I watched as Clara's mother looked in our direction. She nodded at us, a means of acknowledgment.

Clara waved. I waved back. I turned to Tom to hear more, but he was staring at the river, his gaze held to something I couldn't place.

"I keep thinking that I could have been a better friend to Lawrence, that maybe if I had been paying closer attention to what was going on, I might have been able to see things were bad for him, you know, talked to him more about what he was facing."

Clara and her mother walked inside their trailer. I could feel the weight of their steps.

"I did some work in a psychiatric hospital," I said, watching my neighbors. "Some of the folks had really great friends. They'd visit, send cards, call them on the phone." I noticed how the sky was changing around us, the afternoon clouds rolling in like tight balloons.

"The thing is, a person can have all the friends they need, lots of people around them, checking on them, caring for them. But if a person decides they're done with this life, that they've worked at it from every angle they know, if they can't find some measure of peace in the hours of their day, then having a friend doesn't keep them from suicide. It just gives them a name to write on the note before they die."

We stopped talking a little while and watched the horizon. We noticed the dark nature of the coming storm, the shifting of clouds and sun.

"Lawrence really wanted to know every inch of this the land around the river," Tom said, as if I had asked for a memory.

"He stopped by my place awhile back and wanted to know if I had a relief map of the area."

I turned to Tom. "What's a relief map?" I asked.

"It categorizes the differences in height of landforms. I think he was calculating the changes along the river."

"Well, that's odd, don't you think?" I asked.

Tom thought for a minute. "Not really," he said. "Lawrence studied this area like it was a test he was taking. At one time, some years ago, before he heard about the burial site, he thought about buying a piece of waterfront property and putting the community cemetery down here."

"That'd be a little dangerous, wouldn't it, burying folks in a floodplain?"

Tom laughed. "Yeah, that's what he found out. But I know he did a lot of research on the area when he was considering it. He was thinking more of an aboveground thing, a vault, I guess, something that wouldn't be affected by the possibility of floods."

I tried to imagine how anything would really be safe in an area so plagued by water troubles.

"Once he heard the story that there had been a burial ground for some slaves somewhere near here, he began really focusing on making the grounds more permanent."

"That's the story you mentioned that he was interested in?" I asked.

"Yeah. He said he read about it in some old letters, even found out their names. A boat capsized with three families of slaves and most of them drowned, including the captain and the slaveholders, but a few of them survived. The story goes that once they got ashore, instead of running to find freedom, they dragged up the dead bodies of the slaves from the bottom of the river and buried them somewhere near the banks. One of the men who survived was a Franklin."

Tom took a breath.

"Lawrence figured the river had changed so much since those years, the old site was definitely eroded or underwater by now. I was trying to help him find it, but our research never amounted to much. But he kept searching because he wanted to find the place. He thought it was comforting to know some of his ancestors rested near here and comforting to know how far back the family business of undertaking death went.

"He said that regardless of what experts said about mud and a necessary elevation above sea level for proper burial, he thought the riverbank was a good place to lay the bodies of those who had been chained in boats and brought across the ocean. He thought being near the water would help their souls find their way home."

"When's the last time you saw him?" I asked.

"The day before he went missing. We were both getting our cars tuned-up. He was on his way back to the county library because he had found a new clue about the burial site and he was going to check that out. And then he said that the following day he had to go to St. Louis to pick up a body and that he was planning to stay the night, hear some jazz."

"He had plans to be somewhere?" I asked, thinking that it seemed very odd that a person would be getting his car tuned-up and planning a work trip if he was considering suicide.

"Yes," Tom replied. "That's how they knew he was missing. The hospital from St. Louis called looking for him."

"Did you ever find out if his clue led to anything? If he discovered some new information at the library?"

Tom shook his head. "No, I left that morning and was gone until the next day to see a cousin in Fort Smith."

Before I could ask another question about Lawrence, define my interest in him, or consider whether or not he had found out anything about the land around Shady Grove, Clara showed up beside us. She must have come from behind the campers, then snuck around the table, for she suddenly appeared at my side.

"Hey," she said, announcing herself, startling both of us. She had taken off her shoes and was eating a Popsicle. The grape syrup trailed down her arm.

"Hey," I responded, surprised by the sudden arrival.

"It's going to rain," she said. She was studying Tom; her tongue, stained purple, darted across her frozen treat.

"Uh-huh," I agreed and then noticed her interest in who was sitting across from me.

"Clara, this is Mr. Sawyer."

Tom reached out his hand to her. She held the Popsicle tightly and just watched him. He pulled his hand away and nodded at the little girl.

"I've seen you fishing," she said, eyeing him closely.

He replied softly, "Yes, I bet you have." The smile stretched across his face.

"Where are Jolie and your dad?" I asked.

"They're at the hospital," the little girl reported. "She has to stay. We just came to get some clothes."

She finished the Popsicle, put the stick on the table, and wiped her hands down the front of her shorts; the syrup was still smeared down her chin and along the bony part of her arms.

"So, you have to go back then?" I asked.

She nodded. A slow, tiresome gesture, the response of an obedient child, a dutiful sibling. She turned to watch the river darkening in the approaching storm.

And then, I don't know, maybe it was the newness of love, my heart widened by its possibilities, maybe it was the marching of clouds above our heads, the suddenness of atmospheric fluctuation, or maybe it was the sadness of the little girl, so deep within her eyes that it pushed aside the softness of childhood. I'm not sure where the question came from, but I asked.

"Would you like to stay with me?"

Clara didn't answer. She peered directly into my eyes, then turned and ran straight to her camper and inside to her mother. Startled once again by the quickness of her movement, I wasn't sure if she was excited about my invitation or if I simply scared her away.

I glanced up at Tom and suddenly realized I had just altered any plans for us to spend the rest of the afternoon together. I almost apologized for what I had done. But before I could say a word, he stood up, and thanked me for the tea and crackers and, as he called it, "for the polite exchange of ideas."

"It looks like you'll be busy for a while, but if you find yourself without anything to do later this evening"—he turned toward the path behind him, the one beside the pond that went to the quarry—"my place is just on the other side of those hills of rocks." He turned around to face me. "You can't miss it."

I was sure I wouldn't, but before I could say anything in response, I heard the sound of a camper door close behind me. I turned to see that Clara was leading her mother in our direction.

Tom waited until she arrived, made a brief introduction, and then headed to the pond to get his things. I watched him walk away, the sun and everything perfect from the afternoon balanced so easily across his shoulders.

"I'm sorry," the young woman remarked, noticing my attention in Tom's departure.

"No, no," I responded. "It's fine," I added, pulling myself to the things at hand.

"I'm Rose," I introduced myself, leaning up against the table.

"Janice," she replied, "I'm Clara's mother, Janice Miller." She seemed awkward standing beside me.

"Here, sit down, if you've got a minute."

And she stepped around the table and sat down across from me. Clara followed her.

Janice was not yet out of her twenties. She was round-faced, brown as the river bottom, eyes as sad as Clara's. Her hair, darker than her face and eyes, fell just below her chin, and she wore a row of earrings in her left ear. Tiny gold hoops all the way up and around the edge. She held her hands together in her lap. She was hunched, leaning forward as if her heart was too heavy to sit up straight.

"Clara has shown me quite a welcome," I said, beginning a conversation.

Janice smiled. "She's a good girl."

I nodded and the young child grinned.

"She says that you offered to let her stay with you while I go back to the hospital."

"Yes," I answered. "I did."

Then I thought maybe she'd want some information about

me, that a mother didn't just leave her child with a woman she didn't know.

"I'm here for a few days while my car is being worked on."

She turned to see my camper.

"I'm moving west," I said.

"From North Carolina," Clara added.

"Yes," I replied, "from North Carolina."

"We come from Kentucky," Janice reported.

"I told her, Mom," Clara said.

The young mother nodded and there was a pause.

"I guess she told you about her sister then?" she asked. "About why we're here?"

"She just said she was here to see a doctor in Memphis." I wasn't sure how much she wanted me to know, so that was all I revealed.

"St. Jude's," she replied. "We brought her to St. Jude's."

I nodded, realizing then that the pediatric facility was just across the river. It made sense that they would bring the young girl to this area.

"She has cancer," Clara reported. "In her blood," she added.

"Leukemia," Janice said.

"I see," I replied, and then because of my background, I asked. "Lymphoblastic?"

Janice seemed surprised.

"I'm a nurse," I said, explaining. "I worked on the heart unit most of my time, but I did a rotation in oncology."

The young mother nodded. "ALL," she reported.

I knew she meant acute lymphoblastic leukemia, the most

common form of childhood cancer. I also knew it was primarily treated with chemotherapy and that the remission rate was usually quite good.

"I remember the first time I heard the acronym for the disease, "I said. "I thought that ALL must be how it feels for a family when they have to deal with it. All of life becomes affected."

Janice dropped her eyes away from me. I had said too much. There was an uncomfortable silence. The clouds moved above our heads, an awkward dance of shadows and light.

"Would you like some tea?" I asked, trying to ease the stiffness of our conversation. I stood up to go to my camper and retrieve a couple of glasses.

"No, thank you," the young mother answered. "I've already had too much caffeine today."

I sat back down.

"They're going to use my blood to try and make hers stronger," Clara reported.

I smiled. I understood that this probably meant that they were doing a bone marrow transplant, a sign that the standard treatment of chemotherapy hadn't worked.

"When's the transplant?" I asked.

"She went in today for the first part. We thought they weren't going to admit her until the end of the week. They've been running a lot of tests and she's been really weak. But they decided to go ahead and keep her. They started the high dose of chemotherapy this morning. Clara has her procedure tomorrow."

I saw the one tear slide down her cheek. She reached up and quickly wiped it away.

"So." Janice cleared her throat, stopping the run of emotion. "I need to take some things to the hospital."

She pulled her shoulders up and back, a struggle against such a heavy heart, and took a deep breath, gathering her strength. A woman going into battle.

"Frank," she said, looking in my direction, "that's my husband."

I nodded.

"He said that he would stay tonight and then I'll stay tomorrow with both of the girls. My mother's supposed to come this weekend."

"Well, really, I'm happy to spend my afternoon and evening with Clara."

The little girl beamed.

Her mother smoothed back her daughter's hair, thumbing the tiny braids.

"Normally, I would never ask anybody for this, especially"— she hesitated—"a stranger." Then she appeared embarrassed for her words.

"I'm sorry," I said, without knowing what else to say. "I don't blame you for feeling that way; I'd be worried like that, too, if I were you. I know that I am a stranger to you—" I stopped and thought a second.

"I can give you the name of my last supervisor at the hospital or my brother's phone number. They could vouch for me. But really all I can tell you is that I will take care of your daughter."

Janice closed her eyes.

"My head's so full of things I'm supposed to remember—" She stopped, took a deep breath, glancing up at me again.

"Usually, Clara stays with my sister, but since we came to Memphis and she has to be with us to give her blood and do the transplant and my sister has to work—"

"Janice," I said, interrupting her, reaching across the table. "It'll be fine."

I rested my hands near her.

She nodded. And we both knew that I meant only the circumstances of her youngest daughter. I had been a nurse long enough and she had faced disappointment enough to know that no one could make such a grand sweeping promise about the rest of her life.

"Mama," Clara replied in a consoling tone. "I got a cell phone if Ms. Rose gets freaky."

We both laughed, grateful for a simple moment of relief.

"Don't worry about us. You just go and be with Jolie." I felt a drop of rain, looked up and saw that the clouds were about to break.

"We'll be here when you get back."

We paused, the three of us sitting gingerly with her sorrow, and then immediately, having calculated the weight of the storm, we all stood up, taking our leave, and hurried to our campers.

And suddenly, the sky burst open and the rain fell hard, stinging us, a swell of low, hot grief.

TEN

"What color are you?" This was the first question Clara asked me once her mother drove off.

I watched the young woman from the window by the stove as she pulled away from the campground. The rain, though heavy, was just beginning, so the dirt on the driveway and roads was not yet thick or packed. The swirls of dust, like ghosts, stirred behind her.

"I don't know what you mean," I answered, as I poured us both glasses of juice.

She was sitting on the bed, her legs swinging beneath her. She had packed a small bag of toys and coloring books, a couple of movies, before she came over. She was fiddling with the contents as she waited for her drink.

She explained. "I mean, I'm black. My mama is black. The woman with the big dog at the end of the row is white. That man you were with is black." She set the bag beside her and picked at the Band-Aid on the inside of her arm. "What color are you?"

I put up the carton of juice and realized that no one had asked me that question since I was a child. Tight, forgotten memories rushed out.

The dirty names; the ugly looks from the perfectly blond girls on one side of the room and the complete disdain from the dark, angry ones on the other. The questions about my mama's long thick hair and deep black eyes, my father's light complexion. The way I was teased at swing sets and in sand-boxes, called things like "half-breed," or "high yellow," the sticks and stones of children's play. The hard way I learned how to hit.

By the time I was in junior high, I became friends with a girl named Shelley, who was as brown as a hazelnut and as fierce as any boy, and two sisters, Luz and Maria, Spanish, Catholic, and very worldly. With their companionship and loy-alty, I no longer needed the other girls, whose pleasure in-cluded lining up against one another. Once it became clear that it no longer bothered me, I quit being teased and I quit being asked.

I'm sure the mystery of my racial definition crossed the minds of people when, as a young woman and later as an adult, I came into the room where they were, entered into their con-versations, flirted with the possibility of relationships. But no one had asked me in years. I had to think of how to answer.

"Well," I said, gathering my thoughts. "My father's mother, my grandmother, was Irish. My father's father, my grandfather, was black. My mother's mother was full-blooded Lumbee Indian and her father was also white, though not completely, I think."

I sat down at the table by the window. "So, I guess that makes me . . ." I hesitated, trying to figure out how to explain.

"Confused," the little girl replied.

"Yes," I answered, thinking how perfectly a child can name a life. "I would say that's about right."

Clara's question reminded me that my whole life up until Shady Grove had been a struggle with identity. That I never knew where I belonged, and perhaps nothing demonstrated this more than trying to fill out the race box on forms or questionnaires.

I have wrestled with labels and names and categories because I have never known what it has been that defines me the most. Was it my father's defiance of anything other than his whiteness, a prejudice that led him to hate his father and later himself? Maybe it was my mother's longing for a deeper connectedness to her ancestors' earth? The way she kept a small cup of red dirt near her bed, the way she ran through the house, unlocking and opening all the windows and doors?

Was it my grandmother's sad green eyes, her rambling Irish poems of seasides and lost love or my grandfather's broad, thick lips, the son of a son of a son of a slave?

I have never been able to pin down the one thing that soothes my stirred and troubled spirit.

By the time I was out of school, on my own, dating Rip, I was satisfied with my discontent and I wasn't questioned about it so much anymore. I just picked the box that could be most helpful.

If it provided me with financial aid in college or a little bit of an advantage, then I played that minority card. If it meant the consequence of discrimination, applying for a car loan or trying to get an apartment, then I claimed my whiteness.

When we became a couple, I showed Rip the family pictures before he ever asked about my heritage, and I don't believe that it was ever an issue with us. By the time we were married, the darkest members of my family, my father's father and my grandmother Freeman Franklin, the Lumbee, were both dead, so the Griffiths didn't have to share company with them at the wedding or at the social events that brought both clans together. And because I bear more resemblance to the Caucasian side of my ancestry, he and his racist parents just assumed I thought of myself as white. And mostly, I did.

"Never mind," Clara said, noticing the way the question stunned me. "It's not important." She pulled her feet under her, sitting on them. She drank long swallows of her juice.

"Mama says that the color of somebody's skin doesn't tell you anything you really want to know about a person anyway." She handed me the empty glass.

"Yeah?" I asked.

"Yeah," she answered. "It's what you carry inside that matters, the things in your heart," she added, sounding much older than her young years.

I nodded.

The storm blew hard against the camper and we both watched out the window as the rain fell in wide watery sheets; the sky a portrait in darkness.

"What's funny," the little girl noted, "is that on the inside we're all the same color anyway."

I looked at her, unsure of what she meant.

"Our blood," she said, realizing I didn't understand. "Everybody has the same color blood."

"Red," I answered.

"Red," she repeated. And I knew that she had seen enough of her own and her sister's to be assured of this.

A bolt of lightning streaked across the sky. A few seconds passed and then came the large peal of thunder.

Clara jumped.

"Storms scare you?" I asked.

"Just the loud ones," she replied.

Clara is more of a child than I ever was. Even facing all she faced, the sickness of her sister, the complete hold that the disease had over everybody, the demands it made on her parents, her grandparents, on her. The trips to doctors instead of amusement parks, the stays in hospitals instead of hotels, the needles and tests she endured to discover that she was a match for the necessary marrow, all this and so much more than anyone can imagine, and yet she remained so unspoiled, so undamaged by disappointment.

"Why do you think you're so strong?" I asked her after we had eaten bowls of soup and were popping popcorn to enjoy while we watched one of the videos she had brought with her.

We had already discussed the marrow transplant and she understood completely how the procedure went. She knew that she would be put to sleep and that a large needle would be inserted into her pelvic bones. She knew that she would probably be sore in her lower back for a couple of days, that there were risks of complications, but she was not in the least bit frightened.

"Oh, that's easy," she answered.

I waited. The rain was easing up. The storm, just a break from the heat, was blowing past.

"Jolie has an angel."

The microwave stopped and I carefully pulled out the bag and opened it.

"An angel?" I asked.

"Yep," she replied.

I poured the popcorn in a plastic bowl and handed it to her. She reached across the table for the salt.

"Did your sister tell you this?" I asked, taking the shaker from her and using it myself.

She shook her head. "Didn't have to," she explained, taking a handful of popcorn and stuffing it in her mouth.

I sat down across from her, waiting for her to swallow.

With her mouth still full, she added, "I saw her."

I filled up her glass with more juice.

"Where?" I asked.

"Here," she answered.

"Here?" I replied.

She nodded. She was growing a little impatient with my confusion.

"At the river," she said, as if I was not very smart.

"Outside?"

She rolled her eyes and nodded.

"At the tree." She pointed with her chin in the direction where I had seen both her and her sister the day before.

"The angel was in the tree. And when I saw her, I knew no matter what, that me and my sister were going to be okay."

She ate more of her popcorn. I took a few bites of mine. We sat in silence.

"What did she look like?" I finally asked.

"Soft," she replied. "Like a cloud, but not a rain cloud, not like today, like a pillow cloud."

"Right," I said, like I understood, though, of course, I did not.

"And you had never seen her before you came here?"

"I heard her once," she answered, "Jolie was talking to her late at night."

She drank a swallow of her drink. "At home," she explained. "They were talking really low to each other, so I didn't hear what they said. I figured the angel was explaining things to her, letting her know what was happening." She put down her glass.

"But I never saw her until we came here. Until that night I snuck out of the camper and saw her in the tree beside us."

"Was that the night you also saw the man who died?" I asked, remembering what she had said about having seen Lawrence. That he was singing or praying, or something she had said. That he wasn't sad.

She nodded then she shifted in her seat, moving closer to the table. She leaned in toward me to whisper, "I think he saw her, too."

"Where was he?" I asked, trying not to sound too nosy.

"He was farther up, near the edge of the tall grass, near the broken rails," she said, acting as if she was not at all bothered by my questions.

I remembered where I had stood earlier, where I had touched the river for myself.

"And he was down in the water?"

"No, just sort of by the edge. He was singing a song, and I think he was washing off something, like his hands maybe, and he stuck something in his pocket, something red, I think; I couldn't really see what it was." She squinted her eyes as if she was trying to remember.

"Anyway, then he looked up in the tree and he laughed. He laughed like he saw her and knew her or something." She took another handful of popcorn.

"Are we going to watch the movie now?"

"Yes," I said, but not ready to be finished with the conversation. "Did he see you?"

She shook her head. "No." She wiped her mouth with the back of her hand.

I reached for a napkin and handed it to her.

"Just the angel." She wiped her mouth again. "He only saw the angel."

"What happened after that?" I asked.

"He buttoned his jacket and then held out his arms to the river like he was thanking it or something. Then he looked up at the pond like he heard something."

"And then?" I asked because she had paused.

"I heard somebody moving around in my camper, so I

thought I better get back to bed or I'd get in trouble. So I ran inside."

I nodded, trying to imagine how her story played out.

"And the angel floated away," she added. "Just as I opened the door. She flew right past my face, like a piece of silk."

She dropped back against the chair, pulling her bowl with her. "And since I knew that she was Jolie's angel and that she was going to look after us both, I knew everything was going to be okay."

She waited a minute, trying to be patient with me. "Can you put the movie in now?" she asked again.

"Sure," I answered and got up from my seat and moved over to the bed and started the video.

It was the story of a reluctant princess, a comedy, a silly thing, and though Clara said she had seen it already four or five times, she finished her popcorn at the table and then fell on the bed laughing, pulling me beside her.

We watched the entire thing without speaking again of dead men or hospitals or cancer that would not be cured. We watched the entire movie, laughing and holding hands, the wind dying down and the crescent moon rising; Clara fell asleep just as the princess claimed her kingdom and went home.

Janice returned right as I flipped off the TV. I saw the lights of her van pulling up the driveway. I straightened up the camper a bit until I heard the gentle knock on the door. We did not speak to each other, only smiled and nodded as if she had heard and I had spoken all the words we needed said.

I stepped aside as the young and spent mother walked over to the bed where Clara was fast asleep. Janice bent down and gathered her daughter in her arms. I opened the doors for them, first mine and then hers. I followed them into their camper, and as if I had been instructed, pulled down the sheets of the bed, and watched as she laid her youngest child down.

I whispered good night, receiving her kind farewell, and walked outside. Then leaning back against a tree, in the stillness of the night, the river roaring at my feet, I waited for Clara's angel.

ELEVEN

Even though I knew it was foolish to go searching, and even though I was prepared to wait longer than I wait for most people, and even though I prayed prayers I had not spoken aloud in more than twenty years, the angel did not show.

Perhaps, I thought, as I rested against the blessed tree, a steady breeze still stirring from the earlier storm, the stars flickering in the dark, velvet sky, the river a stream of dreams and memories hurrying past, perhaps she is busy watching over the little girl at the hospital or perhaps she is attending to the needs of the recently deceased. Perhaps she has other children to comfort or dead men to deliver. Perhaps the angel wasn't meant for me anyway.

Maybe, I thought, after tasting the wet, sticky air, my neck starting to ache a little from looking up, maybe the angel is only for sick children and depressed undertakers. Maybe the angel, no matter how long I waited at the exact location of her prior

JACKIE LYNN

visitation, reciting Catholic petitions I learned from Luz and her sister in fifth grade and singing old Baptist hymns I memorized from going to church with my grandmother, maybe this angel, or any angel, doesn't just show up when somebody is curious or expectant.

Maybe the angel, like God's good mercy, comes only when you need her.

And yet, as I sat under the tent of birch leaves and summer stars, alone and displaced, it certainly seemed as if I needed her. I had just walked away from the only life I had ever known. I had just said good-bye to family and neighbors, coworkers and friends, and to the places I counted as home. I had packed up and given away everything I owned except for one suitcase of clothes; two cotton towels; a few matching washcloths; a set of sheets; a hand-sewn quilt from my parents' bed; my grand-mother's silver cross necklace; a cigar box of a few family pho-tographs; my mother's wedding band; a pair of crystal earrings that I had won at the state fair; and a set of wine goblets, hand-blown glass ones from Williamsburg, Virginia, sky-blue with red-orange flecks that reminded me of morning.

I sorted and threw out and dismissed and let go of all my trinkets and toys and childhood wishes, my honeymoon pic-tures and my anniversary gifts, my full insurance coverage and the security of everything, I mean everything, I had thought would hold me and keep me and love me until I died.

I bundled it all away in nice neat packages, sending them to thrift shops and secondhand stores. I laid it down at the ceme-tery, in the chapel at the hospital, and at the doorstep of my husband's new home. I packed my life up and left it, signed it all away, and headed west. And as I waited on that summer night, I figured if I ever needed an angel, ever had room in my life for one, it was there at the banks of the muddy Mississippi.

But need her or not, she did not come. But still I waited. The yellow moon rose and steadied. The breeze slipped by. And while I waited, while I counted lights across the river and the things I left behind, I considered what I would ask of the heavenly messenger if she did, in fact, drop by.

I knew that she brought Jolie comfort and Clara confidence. I recognized that she brought the dead man some reason to sing, but I wondered, in the splendor of my summer night, in the flight of my loosed wishes, what gift, what spiritual knowledge would she bestow upon me?

I thought she might bring me clarity in where I needed to go next, wisdom in choosing the correct direction, peace to go along with the notion that I was right to leave my home, right to go searching.

I decided that she would see that I needed strength and courage and insight, that I needed instruction as to where and what I should do next. But even as I named all the spiritual gifts I could use at that particular moment in my life, I realized that if the angel was doing the choosing for what I needed most, if she was selecting the thing that was missing in my spiritual life, then I couldn't be certain that I knew what I would receive. I could not name her imaginings.

But what I did know, what I was fully aware of on that bright, starry summer Arkansas night, that if I could choose, if I could make my own heavenly request, then there would be no doubt as to how I would name the one certain desire of my heart.

Give me back my mother.

Funny, I know, that a forty-one-year-old woman would still long for someone who had been missing from her life for more years than she had been in it, but I did. Strange, I'm sure, that of all things I could pray for, all the things I could use in my life to fortify me, educate me, cultivate me, or illuminate me, that I would ask for that. But I would.

The same thing I have asked of God the Father in brightly lit churches, of his only son, Jesus, while standing on mountaintops at sunrise, of Mother Mary, Divine Virgin, when I walked by the ocean at dusk, of the Holy Ghost when I knelt at my bed, of saints while I drove in my car, and of all the angels I could dream up as I bowed my head before meals. What I have wished on shooting stars every time I saw one, the same thing I have prayed every day since I was thirteen years old. Give me back my mother.

Give me back the mornings of coffee and half a cup of milk and two tablespoons of sugar, of toast topped with sweet cinnamon, browned with too much butter. Give me back those lazy summer days of picking marigolds and sunflowers and black-eyed Susans, filling the shelves in every corner.

Give me back the simple days of working in her garden. Hoeing and raking and pulling weeds. The two of us side-by-side, walking in the long green rows. The sun on our faces, the dirt under our fingernails, the eager moment when I held up a new bean or a tiny wisp of a vine, the way she would smile at me as if I had made it happen.

Give me back the afternoons down at the creek when we threw off our shoes and slid down rocks to walk in clear blue water, when the forest was shady and alive, when she would take me by my arms and swing me up around and around, until dropping me, gently, into a wide soft bed of leaves.

Give me back the late nights of *The Secret Garden* and *Little Women*, of stories of brave men who ran mountains and sailed rivers, who knew the languages of bears and fish and antelope, of women who made baskets from river reeds and wool blankets from tight, twisted yarn, so colorful it hurt your eyes.

Give me back the way I used to fall asleep near her, hearing the softness of her breath. The touch of her hand resting on my head, the easy way she reached for me, pulling me into her, how she always smelled like rain.

Give me back the thoughts of a girl who was never afraid and who never thought of death and who never, ever expected to be left alone in a house with a violent, angry man, in a place that bore no loveliness.

There was no doubt in my mind as I rested on that late Arkansas night along the banks of the muddy Mississippi, dreaming of, waiting for, looking to find some Kentucky child's angel; the only real gift from heaven that I would ask for, the only one I would dream of, hope for, dare to say, would be to know once more how it was to be loved by my mother.

That was the only angel for whom I had ever longed, the only one worth waiting for.

I rose up from the edge of the river, gently sweeping my fingers across the rough birch bark, leaving behind my memories and wishes, my thoughts of heavenly visitors and my unloosed prayers, watching them glide away in the night wind, and I walked. I walked without light or good shoes or a thought or idea in my mind.

And he was waiting for me. Easily, without expectation. And he smiled when I closed his screen door behind me, opening his arms for me as if I were heaven-sent. He welcomed me as if he had known I was on my way and almost there.

We did not speak. We stood in the dimly lit room, holding each other and listening to the sounds of the night, then he led me to his bed. Just before we lay together, standing by his open window, I thought I caught a glimpse of something, a small, gentle thing.

Down by the river, dancing just above the earth, I thought I saw the hem of a garment, a dress, a piece of white wedding silk, the slightest edge of lace. It floated right along the whitecaps of river waves, drifting slowly, such an easy thing to miss. He turned to me and I watched her disappear.

THE
THIRD
DAY

I know he say to trust her
I know he say it fine
But I can see the way she tease
She taking all that's mine.

I know he say he coming
That she bring him down to me
That she take me and my babies
Somewhere we finally free.

I know he say she brown like us
Strong pulse, crooked arm
But I see how she mocks us all
I see she meaning harm.

I know he say be patient
I know he say she fair
But I don't feel no peace for her
I don't think she care.

I know he say to trust him
I know he say it right
But everyday, another day
Sliding dark into the night.

TWELVE

I awoke to the sounds of his reading. He was beside me in the bed; somehow rising without waking me, finding the book and the page he wanted me to hear. I smelled freshly brewed coffee and I heard the sound of his voice just as morning dawned.

" 'The life in us is like the water in the river. It may rise this year higher than man has ever known it, and flood the parched uplands.' "

I lay silently. I was trying to recall exactly what brought me to this place, to this man's side. I recalled the events of the previous night, remembering the talk with Clara and the ache for angels, and how I sat beneath the tree waiting for one to appear. I remembered the strong desire that pulled me from the bank and down the path by the river and into this bed.

Still, I did not speak. Registering my emotions and going over the event, I was letting the peace and the surprise and the delight and the awkwardness all mingle inside me and wash across my spiderwebbed mind. I lay quietly, counting back through those dark hours, the gradual climb to the golden dawn, remembering his wide, tender hands and the arch of his strong, bare back.

I recalled how easily I opened to him, how unafraid and clear I had been as I moved across the shadows of the late summer night, from the tree to the path to his doorstep to his bedroom. I lay next to him listening to his river words and I hardly recognized the woman I was.

" 'Even this may be the eventful year, which will drown out all our muskrats.' " He continued to read. His voice was easy, his pace slow.

Two and a half days from 1420 Pinewood Drive, and already I had taken a different last name, parked my belongings in a place I had never heard of, and was waking to the sounds of a man I had just met.

Rose Burns Griffith, wife, cardiac nurse, timid and orderly, had disappeared somewhere over one of the three state lines I had just crossed and even if I wanted to, I doubted I could call her back to myself.

" 'It was not always dry land where we dwell.' "

I fumbled with my guilt and embarrassment. I had never slept with another man other than my husband before or since the marriage. I had not been in bed with anyone else since I was a child and my friend Shelley invited me to her house for sleepovers. It was strange waking up to somebody I didn't really know, strange feeling so vulnerable, so intimate, so small.

And even though the papers filed in the Nash County Court-house clearly read DIVORCE on them, and even though we had said our good-byes, made our peace, I had not lost the feeling of being tied and belonging to Rip Griffith.

I still felt married and even though I did not regret sleeping with him, it still seemed like a betrayal being in Tom Sawyer's bed, even if I had been the one who was first betrayed. I realized, lying there next to such a slow-talking, kindhearted man, that making love to someone else didn't break the bonds that held me to Rip, that it would take me some time to unloose myself from the wedding bindings.

"It's Thoreau," Tom said, realizing I was finally awake and not quite sure how to greet him. "From *Walden*."

I had not yet opened my eyes, but I could feel him watching me. A breeze blew across us. I heard the river noises, splashing water, the low, soft rumble of a boat engine.

"You okay?" I felt his breath, hot against my neck.

I rolled over and faced him. I opened my eyes. He was smiling. I nodded.

"I'd like to fix you breakfast."

I nodded again.

He waited.

"Read me some more," I said, dropping my face to his chest, sliding myself under his arm.

He held up the book. " 'It was not always dry land where we dwell. I see far inland the banks which the stream anciently washed, before science began to record its freshets.' "

"I've never read him," I said. "We were supposed to read it in high school, but I think I just made up something for the term paper. I never bought the book."

"Then you shall have this copy." He stroked my hair.

I stretched out my legs next to his, pulling the covers close around us.

"I'd always heard that part of the reason he was able to make it out there on that pond by himself was because his sister brought him food, took care of him." I swung my arm across him. "Is that true?"

He leaned himself into me.

"Behind every good man . . ." he said softly.

I knew what he meant.

We were silent again. I could feel his questions.

"I think everybody trying to make it on a pond needs a little help," I said.

"I think you're probably right," he answered.

We listened to the wind in the trees and the calls of birds. We listened to the sounds of our breathing.

"You seem to have done fine without anybody's help," I said.

"I've had help," he answered.

I waited for more.

"I'm an alcoholic," he said quietly, and then added, "with very good sponsors. I have a complete understanding about what it means to rely upon the kindness of strangers."

I lay there considering the life of an addict. The slow hard way through recovery. The three steps forward, two steps back of managing something so much bigger than desire. I thought about Thomas, his regrets, his untold secrets, and wondered from where it was that he had found his strength, from whom he had received care.

"Do you believe in angels?" I asked, thinking about the previous night, about river trees and the edge of white floating in the dark sky.

He was slow in his response, thoughtful. "I suppose I can believe that there's all kinds of spiritual messengers."

I responded only with a nod, my face sliding up and down against his chest.

His bedroom window was open and I heard the passing of another barge, the low purr of hummingbirds diving into his bed of flowers.

"I've never been with anyone other than my husband," I finally confessed, as if it was necessary, as if he had asked.

He put the book down on the table beside us, took off his glasses, and pulled me closer to him.

"Are you sorry about last night?" he asked.

I shook my head.

"No," I answered and then paused. "It just seems odd is all."

I could feel the space opening between us.

"You sleep with someone for most of your life, make love only to them, experience only the way they sleep and breathe and dream, what they like and don't like, what they think you like and don't like, the things you get used to, the things you expect. And then all that's suddenly gone. The life, the love, the way you go to bed and get up every day.

"It's just strange is all."

"This was too soon," he said.

"Oh, no." I lifted my head and faced him.

"No," I said again, even stronger that time. "If anything, it was too late."

I lay back down.

"Rip's been out of the house for two years. And it had been a year before that we had slept together. And it was even longer that he was gone."

I closed my eyes and thought about the way I had become used to feeling lonesome, those last months when we still slept in the same bed, how far away he felt to me as we lay together. He was close enough to reach, to touch, but he might as well have been in another room, in another house, in another town. Once I realized that he didn't love me anymore, I recognized that he had left me long before he packed and moved out.

"I'm just used to being by myself, I think, even though the divorce was just final."

"Getting used to being by yourself isn't a bad thing," Tom said, sliding himself up a little in the bed. "But it's nicer sharing the ride, I think."

His fingers swept across my arm.

"Why didn't you ever settle down?" I asked.

"I was waiting on you," he answered in perfect timing.

I smiled, and even though I doubted he was telling the truth, I liked it.

I liked how it felt on the first morning after we made love. I liked the sound of it and the way he said it, easily and without hesitation. I liked the ring of it, the thought of it, the possibility of it; so instead of pushing for more or emptying the meaning out of it, I just let the answer rest between us. It was all I needed to pull myself through the early surprise of consummating our relationship.

The rest of my time at Tom Sawyer's was spectacular in the most ordinary way. We took showers and ate breakfast. We sat at the table drinking coffee and reading the paper that was left at his front steps. We hardly spoke again, naming only the things we wanted for nourishment.

"Eggs?" "Yes." "Butter?" "Thank you." It was as if we had awakened together and eaten the day's first meal together and greeted the day together for all of our lives.

We were as attuned to how we do things, how we move into the light, how we start our mornings, as any old married couple I had ever known. It was splendid and not at all unusual, and it eased away my embarrassment and softened the clumsiness. It wasn't until the siren of an ambulance blasted through the quiet that we were pulled away from the glory of such a casual hour.

"Sounds like it's close," I said, as Tom lifted his eyes from the paper and stared out the window.

He nodded. "They're on First Street, turning this way," he reported, sounding like a man who knew the town and the roads and the sounds and the traveled directions of folks in West Memphis like he knew his own schedule. "I think they're coming to the campground."

I slid my chair away from the table. "Maybe I should go see," I said, thinking of Jolie and Clara, wondering if the little girl had returned to the campground and then run into some trouble. "Maybe I can help."

He agreed and we both hurried from his kitchen, grabbing shoes and shirts and throwing things on. I headed out the door, planning to run down his path, but Tom called to me and led me around the rear of his trailer where a motorcycle was parked. Quickly, he got on and I followed, jumping on behind him. He cranked it and turned it in the direction of the campground. We looked down at the river sites, but nothing seemed out of place. No one was standing outside. Janice's van was gone and their camper looked locked-up.

We drove on around the driveway and we were at the office in less than five minutes, speeding across the gravel path, arriving a few minutes before the ambulance.

Mary was standing outside in the road. We could hear the sirens getting closer.

"What's wrong?" I asked as I hopped off the motorcycle and ran toward her.

She turned to us and for a moment looked at me and then at Tom, noticing the familiar way we stood near each other. Then she answered with a frantic tone, "Ms. Lou Ellen, she fell beside the desk. I think she broke her leg."

Tom and I ran inside. The older woman was slouched against the wall by the desk. I hurried around the counter. I immediately checked for a pulse. It was weak and fast. Her skin felt moist and cool.

"I've missed my poker game," she said, trying to sound unbothered and without pain.

"What did you do?" I asked, noticing the angle of her right

leg, the hard way it twisted behind her. I knew not to try and move her until the ambulance arrived.

"I got tangled up in the phone line," she said in a bit of a labored voice and then added, "I came tumbling down like the walls of Jericho."

I could see by the position of her legs that she had probably broken a bone. She was pale, breathing very shallow, and I told Tom to get her a blanket or coat to cover her with. He hurried outside to find Mary while I gently slid her down the wall to a flat position and unbuttoned the top buttons down the front of her blouse, loosening her clothes.

Ms. Lou Ellen followed him with her eyes and then she glanced at me and smiled slightly.

By the time he returned with a blanket, the ambulance had arrived and the attendants hurried through the front door followed by Rhonda and Lucas, who were both flushed and wild-eyed. They had gone into town for groceries when Mary had called them on their cell phone.

"Mama!" Rhonda moved past the emergency medical technicians and knelt beside me.

"Darling, I'm fine," she responded weakly. "Just a little crooked."

The ambulance attendants, the same ones I remembered from having seen at the riverside, young people, one man and one woman, stepped beside Rhonda and me, and I moved away from the desk to the front of the counter. I watched as they asked her questions, took her vital signs, and retrieved a small tank of oxygen. Then following thirty minutes of assessment, they slowly and carefully placed the older woman on the stretcher they had brought in with them.

"Mr. Boyd, if we keep having to come out here every week, I may just get me a camper."

The young man was wrapping a sheet around Ms. Lou Ellen while the woman was filling out the necessary forms. Rhonda was answering her questions. The nameplate on his uniform read Cliff Roberts.

"Son, you're welcome here any time," Lucas replied, holding open the door for the attendants and his mother-in-law. And then since the EMT had mentioned it, added, "At least this time, it doesn't seem to be such a grave finding."

I realized then from the conversation between the two men that they were talking about the earlier visit to the area, about Mr. Franklin and finding his body down below the campground.

"That's the truth," the man replied, standing at the foot of the stretcher waiting for the woman to finish the paperwork. He leaned slightly against the door jamb.

"That one was a mess by the time we got to him. He'd been in the water a couple of days, hardly recognized him. Sheriff Montgomery seemed to know who it was right away though."

His partner jerked up and looked in his direction with a disapproving glance. "I think you should radio in the information," she said sharply.

The young man shrugged his shoulders and walked outside. I could hear him talking to the hospital on the ambulance radio.

The woman turned back to Ms. Lou Ellen and was listening to her heart.

"I guess he's talking about Mr. Franklin, the man you pulled out of the river," I noted. "I saw you there," I added.

She seemed to be trying to figure out who I was. "We're not supposed to talk about the investigation," she answered.

I heard the caution in her voice.

"It's being handled by the sheriff's office."

I nodded. I wondered if she had gotten in trouble in the past for discussing cases or if somebody had told her not to talk about this particular one. She turned away and continued listening to Ms. Lou Ellen's heart.

"How are her vitals?" I asked.

The EMT looked at me. She seemed surprised by my question. I could read her badge then and noticed that her name was Becky Kunar. She was pretty, blond, petite, and you could tell she was serious about her work.

"Are you staying here at Shady Grove?" she asked.

"I'm a nurse," I said. "She seemed a little shocky when I came in."

"We'll take her to Baptist," she replied, softening a bit.

"Looks like a broken hip." Then she relaxed a little more. "Blood pressure is ninety over fifty, pulse is thready and one hundred and ten. I think we should hurry."

They put the oxygen mask on her and gently slid the stretcher into the back of the ambulance. Tom agreed to stay in the office and Mary, Lucas, Rhonda, and I jumped into

Rhonda's truck and followed them up the campground road, right on the new loop, and straight up Interstate 55 to the hospital in downtown Memphis.

When we arrived, Rhonda immediately ran to the front desk at the emergency room and registered her mother, who was taken to a room from the ambulance bay. Mary, Lucas, and I headed to the waiting room and sat down together.

"She'll be fine," I said to the two of them as they glanced around nervously.

"The hip is probably broken and that means they'll have to do surgery, but Ms. Lou Ellen is strong and young enough." I leaned back against the sofa. "She'll have to stay in the hospital awhile, but she'll be okay." I was simply making small talk as a means of comfort.

"I tell her every day, slow down, you walk too fast back there. You going to slip."

Mary was upset. I could tell she was worried. "I should have kept her out of office today."

"Mary." Lucas reached over and patted her on the leg. "Dear sister, you and I both know you can't tell Ms. Lou Ellen anything. You couldn't have stopped her from work even if you had known this was going to happen."

Then he sat back and threw his big tattooed arm around her. "This wasn't your fault."

Mary blew out a breath, sliding down next to her friend.

We waited a few minutes and Rhonda joined us. Then she and Lucas went into the emergency department to be with her mother while they continued her care. Mary and I sat alone on the sofa. There were several folks in the waiting area. The television was tuned to a morning news show.

"How long have you been at Shady Grove?" I asked, realizing that I didn't know much about Mary.

"Twelve years now," she answered, glancing up at the television. They were reporting a story about a big wreck near Fort Smith.

"My husband knew Lucas from a long time before." She hesitated, appearing to think about what she was sharing. "They in prison together."

"Oh," I answered, hearing for the first time about Lucas's criminal past, but not being too surprised by it.

"Lucas try to help my husband." She crossed her ankles. "Get him off drugs." She paused.

"Lucas try to help lots of people. Lets them stay at Shady Grove until they find permanent place to live, lets them work for him until he can find them good job.

"He a righteous man. He and Rhonda let me live with them when my husband got picked up again."

Several people walked in through the front doors. A young boy had a bloody rag held against his head. They hurried to the front desk. We watched them.

"I had nowhere else. Roger got killed in prison. Lucas and Rhonda been like family to me." She folded her hands in her lap.

"Ms. Lou Ellen like family, too," she added. "I can't explain it. I have brothers and sisters in Vietnam, where I'm from, but I never feel such love even from them." She paused. "Shady Grove is my home."

A nurse called out a name and two women stood up from their seats and walked to the desk. One was holding her arm gingerly.

"Why is it that Rhonda and Lucas leave the campground so much?" I asked, remembering what Ledford had said when I first arrived in West Memphis and still trying to make up my mind about the couple.

"They have lots of interest," she answered. "See lots of people along the river."

We watched a family leave through the front door. A young woman was being pushed in a wheelchair out into the parking lot. I thought about Lucas's past and how the constant movement sounded suspicious.

"Rhonda can't sleep except on the boat. She say the river calm her, rock her. She don't like being on land, make her feel tight, closed in."

I leaned my head against the top of the sofa and thought about what Mary said. I put aside my doubts and considered that what she said made perfect sense to me even though I hadn't sailed the river. Along the banks of the Mississippi, just to sit on the shore, just to feel the river wind, I had felt my heart expand, the tight strings in my mind loosen.

I figured that a person would feel even more of that kind of experience if she actually floated on top of the water, pushed herself away from land. And I knew that a week before my arrival I wouldn't have understood what Mary meant about Rhonda and about the river, but now I did. After only two days,

I was just beginning to experience my own pull from those muddy waters.

"You and Tom?" Mary asked, using just those words. She stared at me.

I shrugged. "He's a very nice man," I answered, not knowing what else to say.

She nodded. "Good man," she replied. "He had hard time, too," she said, raising some more questions in my mind, only this time they were about Tom.

"What do you mean?" I asked.

"He just been through a lot, lost a lot."

"Lost what?" I asked.

"All his money, all his family's money. Tom been through tough days."

I stretched my neck in her direction, straining to hear more, but Mary just shook her head as if the stories were not hers to tell.

I assumed the financial ruin was related to his addiction and I wanted to ask more questions, but when I glanced up at the front desk I saw the two ambulance attendants who had worked with Ms. Lou Ellen. I dismissed my doubts about Tom and waited until the woman, Becky, left, and then I excused myself from Mary and walked up to the young man.

"Hello," I said.

He looked up and appeared a bit uncertain of who I was.

"I'm Rose Franklin," I introduced myself. "I just came from Shady Grove with Lucas and Rhonda, with Ms. Lou Ellen."

"Oh, right." He nodded. "She's fractured her hip, I'm pretty sure. It'll probably mean surgery."

He signed a paper and placed it with his pen on the counter. "I'm Cliff." He held out his hand.

I shook it. "Yes, I read your nameplate," I said, pointing to the upper right pocket of his shirt.

He peered down. "Right."

"I wanted to ask about Mr. Franklin," I said. "I was there when you brought him out of the river."

He glanced around behind me, looking for his partner, I presumed.

"Do you know who first found him?" I asked.

"Just some fisherman."

I nodded.

"The body was badly decomposed," he added.

"You think he committed suicide?" I asked.

"You family?" he responded.

"Distant," I answered.

"But I'm acquainted with his good friend, Tom Sawyer. He's really upset about the death and I just thought I'd try to get some answers for him."

He nodded as if he understood.

"I don't know if it's suicide or not. It really isn't my place to say. I just put his body in the ambulance. Truthfully though, I think it'll be hard to tell. He had been in there three days. Something had eaten off his ear, he had a lot of cuts and his head had a really large bump on the back of it—"

"Did you check his airways?" I interrupted. I asked this because I remembered working in an emergency room for a summer term in college.

He seemed confused.

"For foam?" I added. "In his mouth or in his nose?"

A drowning victim was brought in and they were able to conclude that he was alive at the time of his drowning because the foam is considered to have formed due to the mixing of air with water. When we wiped it away, it kept returning. I later learned that this was not conclusive, but it still did present important clues to the cause of death.

"Foam?" he replied, as if he didn't really know what I was asking. "No, no foam. But after that much time in the river . . ." He paused.

"To tell you the truth, I didn't really spend much time with the body. Sheriff Montgomery and a few of his men were already there and they just told us to take him to the morgue at the hospital in West Memphis. I only got a real close look at him when we got to the hospital and took him out of the body bag."

I heard his partner, Becky, yell for him from around the corner. Apparently, they had received another call.

"How long was the sheriff there before the ambulance arrived?" I asked.

"I'm not sure, but I think his deputy was with him." He gathered the pen and notebook he had left on the counter.

"So, you don't know how long he had been there before you got the call?" I asked.

He was anxious to get away. "No, but I think it was awhile. He had rolled the body out on the banks. It was a mess at the scene. There were newspeople there by the time we arrived."

He glanced around me.

"One more thing," I asked, knowing he was not going to talk with me much longer. "Did you find anything in his suit jacket when you found him?"

I remembered that Clara saw him put something in his jacket the last time he was seen alive.

Cliff thought for a second. "No, I don't look through the belongings of patients, that's somebody else's job. But I don't remember him wearing a jacket," he said. "Was he wearing a suit?" he asked, seeming confused.

I was just about to answer that I was certain I had seen the victim in a jacket when I saw him on the banks, but he stopped me.

"Look, my partner's through with her smoke break. Ever since she and Fisk got engaged a month or so ago, she's been smoking a lot more than usual. And she rolls her own, takes forever," he said, shaking his head.

"Anyway, we got a call, but I saw that the pathologist from West Memphis is working here today. You could ask him about the foam. It's Dr. Lehman." He hurried past me.

"Thank you," I replied as he turned the corner. I watched as he joined his partner and wondered if he meant Deputy Fisk as the man Becky was engaged to. Then I walked away, deciding a marriage between an ambulance attendant and a lawman was none of my business.

I was walking back to Mary in the waiting room when

Rhonda and Lucas came around the corner. Ms. Lou Ellen had indeed fractured her hip and was on her way to surgery. They were told that we could wait for her upstairs in another area.

We quickly left the emergency department and went to the surgical waiting area. It was three hours before we got word that she was in the recovery room and was doing fine.

THIRTEEN

The surgery was a success. Since it was not a fracture of the femoral neck, but rather a break that occurred farther down, the doctor used a screw that extended across the fracture into the head of the leg bone. The screw was then attached to a plate that stretched down the bone to provide support. This surgery was slightly less complicated than the complete hip joint replacement, and her prognosis was very good that she would be able to return to her normal activities.

Once we received the news, Mary waited for Ms. Lou Ellen in the room she had been assigned, Rhonda and Lucas went for lunch, and without fully understanding what I was doing, I made my way down to the hospital morgue to see if I could find Dr. Lehman, the medical examiner who had pronounced Mr. Franklin dead at the hospital in West Memphis. I wasn't sure why I thought I needed to talk to the coroner, what I planned on asking him, but I sensed a leading from somewhere, a need to know that I decided to honor.

It was a long, meandering hallway from the elevator to the morgue. Like most hospitals, the area where the dead are kept was dark, and cold, and unsettling. I followed signs and directions until I got to the office door of the hospital pathologist. I knocked.

"Yes," a male voice responded.

"Hello," I said as I opened the door.

A man was sitting at the desk.

"Dr. Lehman?" I asked, stepping in.

"Uh-huh." He was sorting through papers. He didn't look up.

"My name is Rose Franklin," I said. "I wondered if I could ask you a couple of questions."

He raised his head. He was an older gentleman with thinning gray hair. He wore glasses and his face was red and splotchy.

"I'm a nurse," I said, thinking that my medical profession might take the edge off what I was going to ask.

He didn't respond.

"A friend of mine, a family member, was brought into the hospital at West Memphis a couple of days ago." I closed the door and moved a little closer to his desk.

"Lawrence Franklin," I added. "He was found in the river."

The doctor didn't say anything. He appeared to be thinking. He put down the papers in his hand and rolled his chair slightly away from his desk.

"The drowning victim was kin to you?" he asked, displaying

a certain amount of surprise that we could be related. Certainly, he remembered the victim was African-American.

"Distantly," I answered, using the same word I had used with the ambulance attendant.

He nodded suspiciously.

"I was just wondering if you concluded whether the drowning was antemortem or postmortem."

I knew it was hard to tell such a thing about a drowning victim and I was sure he wouldn't reveal too much information. I knew the reports were incomplete and that medical personnel are very tight-lipped when it comes to telling family members anything about a deceased relative.

He didn't speak at first. He was studying me.

"I didn't do an autopsy," he answered.

"That's fine. I just thought maybe there were things you could tell about the body."

I shifted my weight from right to left. He obviously was not going to ask me to sit down.

He sighed, appearing to consider whether or not he should say anything about the case. He folded his arms across his chest.

"There was evidence of anserine cutis and skin maceration. A little foam in the airways, some presence of white sand. Several abrasions, bruising, but that, of course, doesn't tell us anything. There was apparent hemorrhaging in the neck muscles, a large contusion on the back of the head."

"And no way really to know if any of those injuries happened before he died or after?" I asked, already sure of the answer, but

JACKIE LYNN

thinking now about the possibility that someone could have hit him on the head and then threw him in the water.

"No, not really." He reached up and removed his glasses, holding them in his right hand.

"The hemorrhage into the neck musculature could have been caused by violent movement during submersion. And any hemorrhage that is leached out of tissues due to submersion creates difficulty in the determination of the time of the injury. He could have been struck after being in the water by a barge or some other vessel."

He set his glasses on the desk and wiped his eyes.

"And the river is full of rocks. He could have hit several as he went downriver. I'm sure you know how fast it moves."

I thought about what he was saying. It was appearing to be more and more difficult that I was going to be able to find out if Mr. Franklin did commit suicide.

He stopped for a second, appeared to be thinking out loud. "In fact, it was surprising to me that he only got as far as he did."

"What?" I asked, not sure of what he had just said.

"The victim is from West Memphis, isn't he?"

I nodded.

"Did they find his car or shoes or anything near where he went in?"

I shrugged my shoulders. "I don't know."

He looked at me surprised, as if I should have that information. He cleared his throat.

"Generally, people who commit suicide by drowning go into the water at a familiar place or at least a place they've been to

156

before. They usually fold their clothes, leave their belongings near where they enter."

His remark stumped me.

"Makes sense," I answered, thinking that it was logical that if the victim was going to kill himself that he would have gone into the river at a known place. I remembered Clara's story about seeing him near the camping site and I wondered if Deputy Fisk had searched the area and if he had found anything of Mr. Franklin's.

"Even if he went in near the bridges, north of town, three days in the river, and he only got a mile down?" The doctor started to relax a little, seemed more willing to discuss his ideas and findings.

"Maybe he got hung up on something?" I said, trying to follow the direction of his thinking, offer suggestions to what might have happened.

"Could be. There's stuff in there that could have held him down."

He seemed to think about what he was saying. Then he added, "But with all these storms, that river has been moving pretty fast."

I paused before asking anything else. I was trying to grasp his line of thinking.

"So, I'm confused," I said, because I was. "You think he wasn't in the water for three days?"

"No, I'm not saying that. His body was very decomposed. He had been in some water for three days. I just question whether or not it was in the Mississippi."

I thought for a minute. "Because of where they found him and where you think he went in?" I considered the question. It was an interesting observation.

"Is there any way to tell? I mean, if he drowned in some other place, would there be some way to tell that it wasn't in the river?"

"Perhaps," he answered, maintaining a tone of interest.

"The river would have a particular content that we could find in his airways, his lungs, even in his bloodstream." He slowed down his pace to explain.

"There are very specific diatoms in the Mississippi. If he drowned in the river, he would have breathed in those organisms that would have entered his respiratory passages along with the air."

He stopped, deciding to give me a full description of his deliberations.

"When a person drowns, they make violent efforts to breathe. Due to this violence some of the alveoli of the lungs rupture, allowing the diatoms in the water source to enter the blood system. If he drowned in the Mississippi, then those diatoms would not just be in his airways, but also in his blood."

"But what if he didn't drown in the Mississippi, what if he didn't drown anywhere?" I asked.

"Then there could still be diatoms in his bloodstream. It's not a conclusive test," he replied, registering a bit of disappointment. "We can have diatoms in our blood for several reasons. And much of the findings that seem consistent with drowning can actually occur with other causes of death. Like the foam in the airways that can come from heart failure or drug overdose."

"So, what you're saying is that you are mostly able to prove if he drowned in the Mississippi, but not really able to prove that he didn't?" I sat down in the chair across from his desk even though he did not offer it to me.

"Right. If he has injuries consistent with drowning, like overinflated lungs, large quantities of water in his stomach, foam, silt or dirt under his fingernails from grasping at the bottom of the river, and the same diatoms in his system that match the diatoms in the Mississippi, then it can be concluded that he drowned in the Mississippi River. If there are diatoms present from another source, then maybe you could prove that he drowned somewhere else, but it would depend on the diatoms and how many places they can be found."

I shook my head. It was a lot of information.

"But what if there are no diatoms in his system?" I asked. "Or what if there are diatoms that are found in the tap water of West Memphis, the same diatoms that you have in your system?"

He smiled, leaning back. "So, now you see why drowning is so difficult to prove." He folded his hands across his lap and continued. "Mr. Franklin could have died in the Mississippi River and gotten hung up on an old piece of wreckage below the surface or on rocks, only drifting a short ways before his body was recovered. He could have accidentally fallen in the water, bumped his head, and died." He hesitated, thinking of possibilities.

"He could have gone in the water for a little swim, gotten in trouble, panicked, and drowned. He could have weighted himself down or taken some medication to slow any reaction and taken his own life by drowning. He could have been whacked on the head, thrown in the water, and died. Or he could have had all this happen somewhere else and then had his body thrown in the river, covering up everything."

I sank back in the chair, trying to take in all of these ideas, recognizing the brick walls we were coming to. There could be lots of plausible explanations for Mr. Franklin's death. And suicide, if what the deputy had said about his psychological state before the death was accurate, was certainly a strong one. I chewed on the inside of my lip. We both sat quietly for a few minutes. Then I remembered something that he said.

"What about the white sand?" I asked.

He interlaced his fingers, sliding his hands behind his head. The wrinkles across his forehead tightened. He didn't appear to remember.

"You said there was white sand in his airways," I reminded him.

"Yes, that's right." He dropped his hands again in his lap. His eyes lit up.

"Is there white sand in the Mississippi?"

He picked up his pen and tapped it against the desktop.

"I don't think there is," he answered, enjoying the idea of solving a mystery. "It's known for the mud, the dark brown mud." He held the tip of the pen against his cheek.

"But there's a lot about that river we don't know," he added. "We'd need to look at it and then compare it to what we find in that region of the Mississippi. It's possible the sand did come from there."

"But it's also possible that it didn't," I added, feeling very much like a detective.

"Did you do the toxicological screens?" I asked, knowing that this would present the most conclusive information.

"No," he answered, putting his glasses back on and placing the pen on the desk next to his papers. He took in a deep breath as if the story was now coming to an abrupt end.

"A deputy came in and said the sheriff ordered them to take the body to Nashville General Hospital. That he wanted a complete autopsy."

"Sheriff Montgomery?"

"The one and only," he replied, with a certain tone of agitation.

"Is that usual?" I asked, thinking the sheriff sure was active in this death and wondering what kind of relationship the doctor had with the lawman.

"Nothing that the sheriff does is usual," he answered. "But to answer your question, no."

He checked his watch. "Most of our medical autopsies are done at the hospital at West Memphis or over here at one of the bigger facilities. If it's a state or federal criminal investigation, they'll send the body to the university hospital in Little Rock."

He scratched his chin and studied my expression.

"I thought it was odd that they sent him to Nashville too, but I figured maybe it was the family's request."

He looked at me as if I had been designated to speak for the Franklins.

I shook my head. "No, I don't think anybody made that request." I tried to sound like I knew the family's wishes.

"Then you'll have to ask the sheriff or the coroner in Nashville. All we have on our records is dead on arrival: death consistent with drowning. Awaiting medical examiner's report."

I stood up from my chair. "Dr. Lehman, I really appreciate all you shared with me today."

I reached out my hand. He stood up from his desk and shook it.

"I just thought of one more thing," I said.

He placed his hands on his desk, bent slightly at the waist, and leaned in my direction.

"Once they brought Mr. Franklin in, do you remember what they did with his suit jacket?" I asked. I was still considering that there might be a clue in his pocket, the red thing that Clara saw or something else he had hidden.

He thought for a minute. "A suit jacket?" he replied in the form of a question.

"Yes, his jacket?" I answered, remembering what the ambulance attendant had said.

"I don't remember there being a suit jacket," he answered. "But, of course, that's not out of the ordinary, if a body stays in that river for three days, there's probably no way a jacket would stay on. The current was just too strong for that."

I was suddenly unsure of the information that I had. I was confident that I had seen a jacket on the dead man, but then I recalled that Cliff, the ambulance attendant, had also seemed uncertain about the garment when I asked him about it.

I paused, considering the pathologist's reply. I decided not to comment.

"Well, thank you again, Doctor. This has been most helpful."

"Best of luck, Ms. Franklin," he said, calling attention to the last name. I even thought he winked.

I smiled, nodded, and walked out the door, shutting it behind me.

I was full of questions as I made my way to the cafeteria to pick up something for lunch. Did Mr. Franklin commit suicide? If he did take his own life, why did he do it? Did Clara really see him down on the river before he disappeared? Why did they take his body to Nashville? Why did the sheriff seem so interested in everything about this death? Why did what he was wearing change from the banks where he was found to the hospital where Dr. Lehman examined him?

And then, of course there was the biggest question of all, why did I care? I quickly ate a sandwich and a salad and then took the elevator up to the floor where Ms. Lou Ellen had been assigned. I followed the hallway until I came to her room. The door was open and I could see that she was in the bed and that Mary, Rhonda, and Lucas were standing around her.

They were holding hands, their heads bowed. And though I didn't see or hear anyone speaking, I presumed that just as they had been doing in the office when I first met them, that they were once again praying. And as I watched them gathered in the room of their loved one, as I sensed their deep concern and common regard, I felt something, something old and sad, deep, and almost forgotten.

I closed my eyes, letting the feeling wash across me as I sorted through the details of the sudden sorrow.

It had been a long time since I had borne the burden of family. I had never had much of an attachment to Rip's people. They were always cold and distant toward me. My dad and I quit being important to each other long ago, and as much as I loved my brother and his wife and children, I never felt at ease with them. It seemed that in our own ways, he and I were trying to escape our childhood memories and when we were together, when we found that shared history in the eyes and tendencies of each other, we were suddenly faced with the stories we were trying to forget. We could never be comfortable in each other's company.

I opened my eyes and watched Mary and Lucas and Rhonda, tears falling down their faces; I saw Ms. Lou Ellen glance up in her postanesthesia state and smile. It was weak, hardly noticeable, but I saw it and I knew that she understood that her child, her child's husband, and her friend, had gathered themselves around her, that they would not let her face her pain alone.

Even in her drowsiness, her surgical confusion, she recognized the circle of grace she was in and she smiled. And I knew that I longed to be a part of that kind of circle, too, longed to be connected, longed to be responsible, longed to know that kind of love. And when I realized that loosed and unbound longing, that old and familiar longing, I also realized why I was suddenly playing investigator with the coroner, why I had so many questions for everybody about Lawrence Franklin's demise, why I was so concerned about the death of a man I didn't know.

It was all related to what I was witnessing in that hospital room, linked to what I experienced when I landed at Shady Grove, tied to what I felt at the banks of the Mississippi River, and connected to my delight in finding love. It was the reason I was drawn to a man who shared my mother's last name, a man who haunted me with his secrets.

A dead undertaker, two ex-convicts, a widowed refugee, a card-playing southern belle, the muddy waters of a burdened winding river, and a man named Tom Sawyer. I didn't know everything I wanted to know about them. I didn't completely trust them, but regardless of what I did and didn't know, I was sure of one thing: I wanted to belong.

I walked into the hospital room, made my way beside the bed, and took the hand of Mary as the three of them continued to pray in silence. I glanced down at Ms. Lou Ellen who had closed her eyes, the smile still spread across her face; I watched a calm, easy nod of approval from her when I joined the circle.

It was crazy, my being here, my thoughts of being a part of this family. It was crazy, my interest in a dead man's dying. It was absurd to fall in love at such a late date in my life and ridiculous to feel settled at a campground.

And yet, as crazy as it was, I welcomed it. I bathed in it. I even prayed over it. Three states over and miles and miles away from everything familiar, holding hands with a woman I had just met, leaning over the bed of a woman I hardly knew, I said a word of thanks. I was finding my way home.

FOURTEEN

Rhonda said that she wanted to stay at the hospital until her mother became more alert. Mary needed to get back to the campground. Lucas went home to get some things for his wife and mother-in-law, and I said that I would come after dinner and stay. I knew that the third shift and the first night after surgery were when my nursing skills would mean the most.

Tom came to get me once Lucas and Mary returned to the campground. He walked into the hospital room, and just seeing him again made me blush. Rhonda raised an eyebrow. By that time, Lucas was the only one who hadn't seen us together and figured things out. As much as a surprise as my falling in love felt to me, it seemed as if it had been anticipated and discussed by everyone else who knew us.

Instead of driving me straight back to Shady Grove, I asked Tom if he would take me by St. Jude's Hospital. I knew it was close by Baptist Hospital and I also knew that it was the day that

Clara was having her marrow harvested. I explained the situation to him, how I had become attached to the little girl and her family and how I figured that since we were in town, I could look in on them and see how things were going.

Tom agreed and dropped me off at the front steps, found a parking place, and said that he would stay downstairs while I searched for Clara's room number and then spent some time with her and the family. He said that he didn't mind waiting for me and that he would enjoy reading the Memphis paper and having a cup of coffee in the coffee shop located in the lobby. He brushed his fingers lightly across my cheek before he walked away. I felt them there while he moved on ahead, felt the kindness long after he had disappeared in the crowd.

I found out that the little girl was on the medical-surgical unit on the third floor. I took the elevator, walked down the hall until I found her room. I tapped on the door and then opened it slightly. She was by herself and asleep. I moved closer to her. There were pillows wedged beside her, keeping her positioned on her right side. Her color was good and I could see that she was being hydrated through an IV line.

She roused a bit as I stood near her.

"Hey, there," I said quietly.

She smiled slightly, appeared a little disoriented. "Hi," she replied, and then closed her eyes again. "Rose."

I sat down in the chair beside the bed and watched her. She slept easily. A nurse came in and checked her lines and her vitals. She nodded at me, but did not speak. It wasn't long after she left that Janice came in. She was carrying two large Styrofoam cups. I presumed she had gone to the cafeteria to get Clara something to drink.

"Hello," I said, standing up next to the bed.

"Hello," the young mother said, looking surprised that I was there.

I walked around and pulled the other chair closer. Janice glanced over to her daughter.

"Did she wake up?" she asked, still holding the cups in both hands.

"Just long enough to say hello," I replied. "She looks good and she recognized me."

Janice nodded and placed one cup down on the bedside table. She sat in the chair closest to her daughter.

I sat down across from her.

"She said she wanted a milkshake," she said.

I nodded.

"When did you get here?" Janice asked, taking a sip from the cup she held.

"Just a few minutes ago," I answered. "I was at Baptist," I explained.

She waited to hear more.

"Ms. Lou Ellen," I said. "Do you know who she is?" I asked, thinking that she might not know the office personnel at the campground.

"Rhonda's mother?" she replied, "The office manager?"

I nodded. "She fell this morning, broke her hip. I was with them in the emergency room."

"Oh," Janice answered. "Is she okay?"

"She had to have surgery, but I think she'll be fine."

"Well, that's good," she said, placing her drink beside her. "Lucas and Rhonda and Ms. Lou Ellen have been real kind to us," she added, then asked, "Did you know that Lucas teaches third and fourth graders at the Baptist church in town?"

I shook my head.

"They give all the money they make to that church or to folks in need," she said this like she knew what she was talking about. "Lets the old folks fish at the pond for free."

I was surprised to hear this about the Boyds, but I was quickly learning that appearances were sometimes deceiving.

The young mother sat hunched in her seat. Her shoulders were rounded and her arms hung uselessly at her sides. She was wearier than when I had first met her the previous day.

"The harvesting go okay?" I asked.

She nodded, a slight smile moved across her face and then slid away.

"How's Jolie?" I asked.

She turned away and breathed a heavy breath. "They moved her to the intensive-care unit this morning," she replied. "The chemo made her sick."

"She has an infection?" I asked, knowing that was a risk with the strong doses they gave before a transplant.

She nodded. "Pneumonia," she replied. "There's some lung damage, too," she added.

I sat quietly. I knew that since Jolie's condition had worsened that they would have canceled the scheduled procedure, and I was surprised that with the changes and the knowledge that the transplant was no longer a possibility, that they would have harvested Clara's bone marrow anyway.

Janice seemed to read my thoughts.

"She's doing this for somebody else," she said, as she turned back around to face me.

I leaned in her direction. "What do you mean?" I asked, confused.

"Jolie can't have the transplant," she reported. "She's too sick."

I nodded. I had figured out that much of the story.

Janice reached up and pushed a strand of hair away from her daughter's eyes.

She waited and then sitting farther up in her chair, she explained, "Clara said that last night she had a dream."

The little girl stirred and we both watched her. She raised her head a bit, but then dropped it down again, still asleep.

Her mother pulled away from Clara and spoke in a quieter tone. "She said that an angel told her that Jolie"—the young woman stopped and began again—"that her sister wouldn't need the blood where she was going." She took a breath.

I reached across the bed and took her hand.

She hesitated, and then continued. "That she would be fine now in her new place without the transplant, but that there was another child, a little boy down the hall from Jolie, who would need it, who would stay here where he could use it."

Then a few tears fell and the young woman dropped my hand and I could tell she needed a tissue. I handed her the box that was beside the bed. I didn't know how to respond.

I knew that if Clara was right then she was saying that her sister was going to die. I tried to imagine how her parents were taking this news, how such a conversation occurred among the family members, how a mother answers a daughter bearing such a painful insight.

"When did she tell you this?" I asked.

"This morning, on the way to the hospital." She dabbed her eyes with the tissue. "I didn't believe her. I told her that it was just a dream and not to worry, but then when we got here, the doctor came in and told me and Frank that Jolie wouldn't be able to have the transplant."

She wiped her eyes and then placed her hand on her daughter's leg.

"And Clara asked the doctor about a little boy. She asked him if there was somebody else who could use her marrow."

I waited and then asked, "And was there?"

Janice nodded her head slowly while she watched her daughter.

"A baby," she answered. "He came in yesterday."

She leaned forward and picked up her cup. She took a sip.

"The doctor checked the list of patients and sure enough she was right. The baby, who also has ALL, was a match with Jolie and Clara." She shook her head as if she still couldn't believe it.

"The family came here from the mountains somewhere. The staff had been searching the donor register all night." She put down the cup.

"It's a rare match," she said and drew in another deep breath.

"Clara wanted to go ahead and do the procedure this morning."

I glanced over at the little girl, wondering how she could have possibly known about her sister, about the baby down the hall, wondering how children can know so much more than the rest of us.

She stirred again and this time opened her eyes. Janice stood up from her seat and knelt near her. "Hey, sweetie," she said.

"Hey, Mama," she answered. Then she turned in my direction. "Rose came to see me."

Janice smiled and glanced at me.

"Yeah, darling, I know. We were just talking about you." She rubbed the little girl's forehead.

"Did you tell her about the angel?" she asked.

Janice nodded. I stood up next to her.

"And she told me how brave you were and how kind you were to give your marrow for that little boy," I said, gently stroking her arm.

She closed her eyes. "Jolie told me to," she answered softly. She yawned and then grimaced as if she felt a twinge of pain. A moment passed and her face softened.

"She came to me, too, with the angel last night. She told me about the baby." She opened her eyes, looking around the room as if someone had called her and then she closed them again.

Janice and I returned to our seats. The room fell silent. I tried to understand the details of the morning, tried to figure out the mind of a child. The young woman finished her drink.

It wasn't more than a few minutes later that two nurses came to the door and called Janice outside. I could tell from their demeanors, the way one woman put her arm around the young mother, the awkward way the other stood watching, that something was wrong, that Jolie's condition must have worsened.

I heard their low conversation and then footsteps hurrying down the hall. No one returned to the room.

I reached over and took Clara by the hand.

She opened her eyes.

"Jolie and the angel are together now," she said.

I squeezed her fingers and nodded.

"She'll be happy," the little girl said, dropping off to sleep, a tear in the corner of her eye.

I sat in the room while she slept, watching her chest rise and fall, her face wrinkle and relax, and I wondered if the angel and her sister had stopped in this room on the way to wherever they were going, if Clara was hearing a message from the other side, if in her sleep she was being comforted in her loss.

I wondered if there would be enough solace from an angel and a child to soothe the hard ache in a husband and a wife, fill the empty place in the hearts of a mother and a father, if there was ever enough relief to ease such grief.

The doctor came in and checked Clara. A deep sadness had fallen across his face. A chaplain visited and prayed in silence. Nurses came and went. All of them trying to assess that the little girl was okay. All of them concerned with how she would take the news about her sister. And all the while she slept, an easy rhythm of breath and dream.

I waited with her until her parents returned to the room about an hour later and then I left them alone. They were broken, of course, overwhelmed in their sorrow, but they remained steadfast, appeared resolved, somehow at peace as they stood at the foot of the bed of their daughter, who had bridged so carefully the stories of life and death.

On my way out, as I headed down the hall, I met a couple walking hand in hand toward Clara's room. I knew when I saw them that they were the parents of the baby who had received the little girl's marrow, that they were the recipients of an angel's good wishes. And I thought once again of how deeply we are all connected, how much we rely upon one another.

I found Tom in the waiting room and we walked to the parking lot without speaking. He didn't ask me anything as I let the tears fall. I held on tightly to him as he drove us across the bridge to West Memphis. I held on tightly to the depth of feeling I had uncovered in hospital rooms and to the lessons I had learned.

I held on tightly to what it was I knew I had to do. I wanted to ease the grief of Tom and I wanted to solve the mystery of his friend's death.

As we exited near the foot of the bridge, I told him of the next stop I knew I had to make.

FIFTEEN

Ms. Eulene Franklin, widowed and now once again bereft since the loss of her oldest child, her only son, was sitting in the kitchen shelling peas when Tom and I arrived. She was a small-boned woman, bent from age and stooped from long hours of work standing over sinks and garden tools. She had a row of braids around her head, all ending in white pearly knots, tiny wisps of hair falling out of the plaits.

"She's blind," Tom whispered to me, as we knocked on the back door of the old wooden house that stood at the corner of Second Street and Pine, right across the road from the offices, chapel, and workrooms of Franklin's Family Funerals and beside an empty lot overgrown with pigweed and clover.

"Ms. Eulene," he called out as he pressed his face against the wire mesh of the screen. "Ms. Eulene, it's Tom Sawyer."

I heard a chair slide across the floor. "Who's that?" a voice replied.

"Tom Sawyer, Ms. Eulene, from over at the river."

She shuffled across the floor to the door, pulling it open. She wore a flowered housedress and a faded apron. She had on bedroom slippers and dark glasses.

"Thomas? That you?" she asked as she stood in front of us.

Tom reached up and touched her on the inside of her arm. "Ms. Eulene, how are you today?" he asked as if had he visited her recently. He kissed her on the cheek and she wrapped her free arm around his waist.

"Thomas Sawyer," she said. "You know your mama just left not more than twenty minutes ago." She held open the door and we walked through. "I should have known that was you on that bike. I can hear you coming four miles away."

She turned her head to the side when I walked in. She recognized that Tom wasn't alone. She waited for the introduction.

"Ms. Eulene," he said as he stood by her side. "This is a friend of mine. This is Rose."

I grasped the back of her hand.

"Ms. Eulene," I said, stepping closer to her. "It's so very nice to meet you."

She raised her chin and then reached up and touched me on the cheek. She dropped her hand, smiled slightly, and then moved away from the screen door and it closed behind us. "Nice to meet you, too," she answered.

"Well, do come in, here, take a seat." She shuffled toward the table and pulled out a chair. "I was shelling some peas that Audrey Timmons brought by."

Then she waved her hand toward the counter. "Have you

ever seen so much to eat?" she asked. Her voice was tired, but in spite of how it stretched, she was trying to sound upbeat.

I glanced over and she was right. There were pots and pans and dishes pushed in long rows along the countertop. I wondered how she would remember everything that was there.

"People been bringing me food for almost a week," she said as she moved over to her chair. "I don't know why they think I can eat all that." She eased herself into her seat, holding onto the table until she got all the way down.

"Rose, here, sit down over here." She pointed to the chair beside her.

I walked behind her and sat down at the table.

"Thomas, I want you-all to have a plate of food before you leave," she said. She sounded like a mother speaking to her children. Even lost to her grief, I could tell she was a woman used to taking care of others.

"Yes, ma'am, we will do that." He winked in my direction.

She pushed a bowl of peas away from her and rested her hands on the table. Another bowl was situated between her and Tom.

"You by yourself?" Tom asked.

"Uh-huh," she hummed. "Rusty went over to the office. She's trying to get things arranged over there."

"Rusty is Ms. Eulene's neighbor," Tom said to me as an explanation.

I nodded.

"Beatrice's daughter, she stays here with me," the older woman added. "Lord, I don't know what I'd do without her right now." She reached in the pocket of her apron and took out a tissue. She wiped underneath her glasses with it and then kept it balled-up in her hand.

"Rose, are you visiting West Memphis?" she asked.

"Yes, ma'am," I answered. "I came from North Carolina."

"North Carolina," she repeated. "I got people in Raleigh," she said.

"I'm not too far from there," I responded. "I'm from the eastern part of the state, Rocky Mount."

She nodded.

There was an awkward pause. She waved away a fly that was buzzing around her.

"I'm real sorry about your son," I finally said.

She lifted her face slowly. "Thomas tell you about it?" she asked.

"I was at the river when"—I stopped, not sure of how to continue—"when they found him."

She dropped her head in her hand. "Just don't seem right," she said softly.

Tom reached out, placing his hand on her shoulder.

She rocked in her chair, back and forth.

"I knew there was trouble when he didn't call me before lunch the day he was supposed to be leaving St. Louis," she said, as if she was trying to order the tragedy, trying to understand the sequence of events leading up to her son's death. I was sure she had already done this several times since his disappearance.

She pulled the tissue out again, pressing it against her wet cheeks.

"I told my neighbor, Beatrice, about eleven o'clock that

morning that something had happened. I just felt it. I just felt it here." She pointed to her heart.

"Then I called Rusty at work and I got her to call his phone." She rolled the tissue in her hands. "There was never any answer."

She shook her head.

"By the afternoon I got hold of the sheriff. I told him that I just knew Lawrence was in some kind of trouble."

Tom patted her on the arm.

"I know, Ms. Eulene," he said. "Once I got back from Fort Smith and after we heard from St. Louis that he hadn't made it to the hospital, we were all out looking for him by dinnertime."

She turned away, still moving her body in a rocking motion.

A car passed on the road outside the house. She lifted her head as if she was listening to see if it was somebody stopping. It came to the intersection and turned toward town.

"Now they're trying to say Lawrence took his own life," she said the words painfully. "It's just ugly how folks talk," she added.

We sat at the table while she wiped her eyes again. Tom and I looked at each other without knowing what to say to the older woman.

"Ms. Franklin," I finally asked, even though I knew it wasn't my place, "why would they say that about your son? Why are they saying he committed suicide?"

She bit the inside of her bottom lip, shaking her head. "He was on some medicine," she answered.

"For depression?" I asked.

"No, he told me it was to help him to sleep," she replied.

"He was under a lot of stress trying to run the business by himself."

She turned toward Tom. "You know, Thomas, it was too much for one man. I tried to get him to get some help and he had gone to visit a cousin in Louisiana about coming to West Memphis, but he liked to do things by himself. You know, Thomas," she said again.

"Yes, ma'am," he answered. "He was a hard worker."

She nodded her head.

I pressed for more. "Was there any other reason they would say he took his own life?" I asked.

She turned in my direction. Her brow wrinkled as if she was studying me. "Who did you say you were again?" she asked.

"My name is Rose," I replied, knowing I needed to explain. "Rose Franklin Griffith," I added.

She chewed on her lip. "Did you know my son?" It was a legitimate question.

"No, ma'am." I knew I sounded suspicious.

"You working with the police?" she asked. She had obviously already been questioned by Montgomery or one of his men.

"No," I answered.

I could tell she was trying to figure out why I was asking so many questions. I knew I needed to explain why I was there, but I knew that at the time I didn't fully understand that myself.

"I just keep thinking about him, about my coming on the day he was found, about why he might have taken his own life."

I changed positions in my seat. I felt uncomfortable trying to talk to the grieving mother.

"I feel like something's wrong about what they're saying about Lawrence, about his death—" I stopped.

I crossed and uncrossed my legs. I could feel Tom watching me. I knew that he was curious, too, about my desire to meet Mrs. Franklin, about my sudden questions for her.

"My father and I are not close." I felt as if I was going to have to start at the beginning. "I have a brother, but we don't really talk. My mother died when I was a little girl. I've just gotten a divorce and I wasn't even planning on stopping here." I looked at Tom. This was for him, too.

I shook my head, started again. "I met a little girl at Shady Grove, at the campground where I'm staying." I added, "Her name is Clara and I've talked to her a few times now."

I slid my hands together and then pulled them apart, placing them on my legs. I was quite uncomfortable. I felt the scrutiny of the older woman and of Tom.

"She said that she saw Lawrence sometime the night before or the morning that he disappeared, down at the river." I cleared my throat and continued. "She said he was happy, that he laughed and that—" I stopped again, knowing that I was starting to sound a little crazy. "She said that there was an angel there."

Neither Mrs. Franklin nor Thomas spoke.

"I don't know how to explain it," I said, fidgeting. "I just feel like something's not right about what they're saying about your son. I think somebody's covering up something; I don't know why, but I think I'm supposed to figure it out."

The older woman made a low humming noise like she was

thinking, studying on what I was saying. I figured she was going to ask me to leave or just be polite and halt our conversation.

"What was your mama's name?" she asked, surprising me with her question.

I answered her truthfully. I knew she deserved to be able to ask me anything after my questions about her son.

"Rose Pearl Franklin," I said. "I was named after her."

"Rose Pearl," Ms. Eulene repeated. She interlaced her fingers and rested them on the table. She had stopped rocking.

"Are we related?" she asked.

I dropped my face. "I don't think so," I replied. "I didn't know my mother's people, but they weren't—" I paused, not knowing how to talk about race. "Her mother was Lumbee Indian. I never really knew about her father. He was the Franklin and I think he was from Georgia or somewhere south. I never knew any of his family."

The older woman smiled slightly. She unfolded her hands and reached over to take mine.

"It don't matter," she said. "We all mixed-up anyway." Then she pulled her hands away and stretched her back so that she sat up tall in her seat.

"Lawrence would never have committed suicide," she said sternly, matter-of-factly.

"He respected life, honored it. People think that because he was an undertaker that he resigned himself to death, lay down to it, but they didn't know my Lawrence. He never stopped death when it came to this community; he knew we all got a time to go and he helped a lot of others make their way to the other side." She spread her fingers on the table, wide like she was playing the piano.

"But he would never have sent himself or somebody else across the Jordan if it wasn't time." She folded her fingers into fists. "And I know it won't his time."

We heard steps on the front porch and a young woman of about twenty walked through the door. She smiled at Tom and looked at me. The door opened and closed.

Mrs. Franklin listened to the sounds at the door and to the sounds of the woman coming into the room. She waited until she was just in front of the sink. "Rusty, this here is a cousin of mine, Rose Franklin."

I was stunned at the older woman's description of who I was. I felt my face flush.

"She's visiting from North Carolina. She's a friend of Tom's." She reached over and knew right where my hands were placed. She took one in hers.

"I'm happy to meet you, Rusty," I said.

The young woman lifted her eyebrows and smiled. "Nice to see you, too," she replied.

"Ms. Eulene hasn't fed you yet?" she asked, walking over. She placed her hands on the older woman's shoulders and squeezed them lightly.

"In time," Mrs. Franklin replied.

"Well, I just came to check on you. I'm going to go back and get some folding chairs to bring over. I figure that we'll have a lot of people here again tonight."

She turned around and seemed to be taking inventory of the

food on the counter behind us. She lifted foil and plastic wrapping, studying the contents of the containers.

"You need some help?" Tom asked, as he stood up from the table.

"Yes, thank you, Mr. Sawyer, it would be nice to have an extra set of hands," the young woman answered, still sorting through the food.

I started to get up, too. She turned around.

"No, Rose, it's okay, you stay here. It won't take us very long," she said.

I sat back in my chair and watched as Tom and the young woman left the kitchen. I followed them with my eyes as they walked across the road. Mrs. Franklin hummed quietly.

"You want me to help you with these peas?" I asked, remembering that she was involved in that activity when Tom and I arrived.

"That'd be pleasant," she answered.

I slid the two bowls that were on the table near us, placing the one with the unshelled peas and hulls in front of the older woman and setting the one with the finished peas closer to me. I took a handful of shells, placed them on the table, and watched the older woman as she sifted through the bowl.

"You grow up with a garden?" Mrs. Franklin asked.

"Yes, ma'am." I answered. "But it's been a long time since I worked one." I fidgeted with a shell.

"Yes," she replied. "Me, too. The plot is a mess now," she added, and I knew she meant the lot next to the house that I had seen when we arrived.

"Junior," then she noted quickly, "that was what we called my husband. Junior always plowed the land for me. And then Lawrence did after his father died." She stuck her thumb in the end of a long shell and slid it down. She made it look so easy.

"It's been a few years since I had a vegetable garden," she added. She felt around for the bowl and then slipped the peas into it. She dropped the hull in the bowl in front of her and picked up another. "Just got too hard."

I watched her work. I found the string on the seam of the shell I was holding and pulled it down. Then I stuck my thumb inside and tore it open. Peas fell out. I thought I saw Mrs. Franklin smile as if she had seen what I had done. I picked up the peas and placed them in the bowl.

"Mrs. Franklin, did Lawrence write a letter before he died?" I asked. I remembered what the deputy had said.

"He wrote some things down that's all." Her fingers moved like a typist at work. "I told them he was doing that before his birthday, that he always did that, made an inventory of things, wrote notes for people, cleaned out closets. His birthday is in a couple of weeks and he did that every year. It was just his way of ordering the years of his life." She blew out a breath.

I didn't respond. Lawrence's actions made perfect sense to me, but I could see how the police would try connecting those things together to call his death suicide. It was logical in their minds. The two of us kept working at the peas.

"Did Lawrence ever mention anything to you about river property or trying to find something down there?" I was still trying to understand her son's life as well as his death.

"Lawrence loved that old river." She smiled. "He was always reading about the history of it, trying to figure things out about it." She moved quickly through the hulls. She was so much faster than I was.

"He wanted to put the cemetery down there." She laughed a bit.

"Junior told him a long time ago that it was crazy, but he just had this notion in his head." She slid and pulled another row of peas into the bowl.

"That was when he started all his reading, when he found about the old slave burial grounds."

"Yes, Tom mentioned that."

"Lawrence was real serious about it. He wanted to find it, thought it should be a historical landmark or something." She let out a breath.

"Went down to the courthouse trying to get somebody to help him search for it." She shook her head.

"How long ago was that?" I asked.

"Oh, I don't know." She seemed to be thinking about the question. "I guess it was a year or there about." She paused again.

"Did he get any help from the city? Did they ever find it?" I asked.

"Nah. The city manager said that it couldn't be any burial ground near the river, that he must have had his locators wrong."

She slid a hull apart. "He gave up on it after a while."

I reached for another shell, a long firm one. I opened it and spilled the peas again, this time on the table and on the floor.

"Until a couple of weeks ago," she said.

"What?" I asked.

"He brought it up again at dinner a couple of weeks ago," she said.

"Brought what up?" I asked, scooping peas from the floor.

"The burial ground." She reached around the bowl for more shells. She had done ten or twelve and I was still working on my second.

"What about it did he bring up?" I asked curiously.

"Just that he thought he had figured out where it was."

I faced the older woman. I had quit shelling by then.

"Was it near Shady Grove?" I asked.

She thought for a moment and then nodded slowly. "I believe it was," she answered. "But not right at the camping sites," she added. "I think that he thought it was closer to the quarry, closer to Tom's."

She reached her hand in the bowl and let the peas slide through her fingers.

"It looks like we finished," she said.

"It looks like you finished," I replied. "I just made a mess."

I glanced around the floor for more peas that I had dropped.

She reached over and patted me on the hand. "You did fine," she responded. "There wasn't too many left to do anyway."

"Mrs. Franklin"—I thought since we were talking so openly about her son I had room to ask more questions—"did Lawrence ever mention anything about the slave's gold?" I knew it seemed to be an unrelated question. I just thought that the story that Tom had told me might be connected to the death.

"No. I mean, everybody knew that old story; Tom knows more about it than anybody, but Lawrence and I never talked about it."

She brushed the tiny pieces of strings and hulls from the table, sliding them into the cup of her hand. "It wouldn't have mattered though." She dropped them in the bowl of old shells.

"Why not?" I asked. "If it's true what folks say, that the gold was buried somewhere on this side of the river, it would be worth a lot of money. I would think somebody might be interested in finding it."

"Oh, I didn't say somebody wouldn't be interested," she replied. "I'm just saying Lawrence wouldn't be interested."

"Why?" I asked again.

"Lawrence felt like a lot of the black people around here feel. They understand that gold was meant to buy their flesh. Not too many south side people would go looking for that kind of sorrow. And besides, Lawrence never cared anything for money. Just wasn't something he thought about."

She placed her hands in her lap. I felt embarrassed that I would have implied that her son was looking for tainted gold. I recalled that Tom had said something very similar to what the dead man's mother said. I waited for a minute and then asked, "What did he care about?"

I was still curious about the kind of man he was.

"Family," she answered. "He was interested in family and how we were all related."

She smiled slightly.

"He'd have known by the end of the day how we were connected. He would have searched through his papers and been able to tell you by supper time how your mama's people and the Arkansas Franklins were kin."

She found another tissue and wiped her eyes. I felt a little sorry since I felt as if I had caused the tears.

"He traced every family's history in Crittendon County," she said. "At least the ones living on the south side," she added.

I knew she meant African-Americans.

"It's hard sometimes finding the histories of slaves," she said as she touched the sides and back of her head, sliding in the pieces of hair that had fallen out of the braids.

"Yes, ma'am," I answered. "I think it would be."

"Lawrence was happiest when he would bring families together, when he could bury relatives near each other."

I nodded, then realized she couldn't see me. "Yes, ma'am," I said again.

"That's why he wanted to find that burial ground," she explained.

I listened more carefully. "What do you mean?" I asked.

"Lawrence found the names of the people who died there. They were written in an old Bible of a man who died some time ago. The family gave it to Lawrence when he was writing up the obituary for the paper. He found the names on a page just in front of the Old Testament; once he realized that some of the names were the same as people living in West Memphis, he wanted to find and mark the site, give honor to the dead people who rested there. He found out that it was his great-great-great-grandfather, or something like that, who had been the one to bury those slaves."

She paused for a minute.

"Did Thomas tell you that story?" she asked.

"Yes, ma'am." I remembered my conversation with him from the previous day.

"Well, Lawrence thought he owed it to the community to find that cemetery. He thought he owed it to his ancestor, to his great-grandfather, to his grandfather, to his father, to honor what had been done, to mark their lives, to name their passing. To say to this community, to these families, here are your ancestors, your roots. Our blood flows from them."

She stood up from the table and took the bowl of peas to the sink.

"Lawrence cared about family," she repeated. She turned on the water and began washing the contents of her bowl.

I watched the blind woman as she sorted through the small brown peas, able to pull out string and dirt, the easy way she read the vegetables with her fingers. She hummed a bit while she stood with her back to me. I saw Tom and Rusty coming across the road with their arms filled with folding chairs. He was laughing at something the young woman was saying. Delight spread wide across his face. I watched the way she flirted with him, the way he seemed to enjoy it.

"Mrs. Franklin," I asked, because the thought had just crossed my mind. "Did Lawrence tell anybody else that he had figured out where the grave site was?"

She faced me and nodded like she was thinking. Then she turned off the water. "Well, let's see, I know he told the old man who leases the land from Mr. Boyd for the quarry rights, a Mr. Koonerd or Cunley. He told the Boyds, too, because I think Mr. Boyd let him go over from time to time to look at the place. He told me at supper when Beatrice and Rusty were here, I believe. Thomas knew, of course, because they had been working on that cemetery project together." She sifted again through the peas. "And that's right, he told Sheriff Montgomery."

The name made me jerk toward the older woman. "Why did he tell the sheriff?" I asked, thinking that I was hearing his name far too many times.

"He was on his way to the courthouse to look at the land deeds. He said he ran into the sheriff on his way in and that when the sheriff asked about what he was doing there, he mentioned it to him." She set the bowl aside and wiped her hands.

Tom and Rusty had walked around to the front door and were bringing in the chairs. I could hear them opening them and setting them around the room. I heard them mention the preacher, and that the family didn't know yet when the service was going to be held. I could tell by the awkward silence that followed that it remained a subject of displeasure for the family and friends of Mr. Franklin.

"He said the sheriff seemed real interested in his findings, said he thought the city ought to mark it like Lawrence wanted. He even said that the sheriff told him to keep him posted about it because he wanted personally to make sure the historical society took the request seriously."

"Have you seen the sheriff?" I asked, not sure why.

She nodded. "He was the one who brought the news to me, gave me Lawrence's jacket."

I suddenly realized why the victim was not dressed the same way he had been down at the river once he arrived at the hospital, but I still wondered why the sheriff had taken the garment.

I didn't think that was usual, to take things from the scenes of crimes and deliver them to family members. Hearing this news made me even more suspicious about the sheriff. I wondered if he had been searching for something.

"Did anybody find anything in the pockets or on the jacket anywhere?" I asked, not knowing what there might have been to find.

"I didn't hear if they did," the older woman answered. "I just put it in there on the desk," she said. She could tell I was still interested.

"You can go look if you want," she added, and pointed with her chin to the room next to the kitchen.

I headed in the room and saw the soiled jacket placed upon the top of a desk. It had been ripped in places and was muddy. I searched in the two front pockets. I found nothing. Then I reached into the pocket on the inside of the garment and felt a hole.

When I stuck my finger into the hole I was able to feel a narrow piece of material stuck inside the lining of the jacket. It was smooth and felt wound together. I pulled it out and immediately recognized it as red ribbon. It must have been the red item that Clara had mentioned seeing him put in his pocket.

"Mrs. Franklin." I walked back into the room where the older woman was standing by the sink. "Do you know what this is?" I asked.

I placed the object in her hands. I watched as she slid it through her fingers from end to end, rolled it around on her palms. She shook her head.

"Well, no. It feels like a ribbon of some kind," she replied.

"I think it is a ribbon," I answered.

"Is that right?" she asked. She handed it to me.

"What color is it?" she asked.

"Red," I answered.

And she nodded as if she knew exactly what it was. She turned back to the sink.

"It's marking ribbon," she noted. "Lawrence and his father used red ribbon to mark the graves for the gravedigger." She placed one of her hands on top of the other. "He probably just had it in his pocket from the last burial," she added.

I thought she was right. I knew I was forever finding things in my pockets that I had stuck in there while I was at the hospital. The ribbon had more than likely been in there for sometime and had nothing to do with his death.

"I'll just put it back," I said. I could tell the finding had upset her.

She just made a low humming noise, as if she was recalling an old song.

I returned to the room and placed the ribbon back in the dead man's jacket.

When I made my way to the kitchen, Tom was walking into

the room. Mrs. Franklin heard him come in and turned toward him and the young woman he had been assisting.

"Now, Thomas, I want you and Rose to fix you a plate of food before you go," she said as she placed the towel beside the sink, trying to sound upbeat.

He moved near her and hugged her tightly. "I already told your neighbor that I will make sure we get something to eat," he replied. Then he stepped away from her and stood beside me at the table.

"We won't go away hungry," he added, standing close enough that his arm brushed against my shoulder.

And we didn't. We spent another hour at Mrs. Franklin's house, eating plates of ham and biscuits and potato salad, speaking of easier subjects than death and sorrow. We had big pieces of chocolate cake for dessert, and once the bereaved woman heard the story of Jolie and Clara, and heard about Ms. Lou Ellen's accident, she made Rusty wrap up some of the food on the counter to take down to the campground.

"Rose Franklin," the older woman said after Tom and I made several trips out of her kitchen and to her neighbor's car. We had said our good-byes and were walking out the door for the final time. "You are welcome in this house anytime." She grabbed my hand and squeezed it.

"Thank you," I said, and knew that I was.

Tom and I followed Rusty to Shady Grove, and when she stopped at the office to drop off the food, we pulled in behind her. As I got off the bike I looked down at the river and saw the police car parked by my camper.

We unloaded Rusty's car, speaking only briefly to Mary, who hurried around trying to clear off a space for all the dishes. Tom mentioned that he needed to drive into town to the courthouse, that he had asked for some copies of something he was studying and that he would be gone only for a couple of hours and then would drive me back to the hospital.

I told him that I would walk the rest of the way and I watched as he drove down the path toward his home.

Once Rusty left, I headed to the river. I knew my chance to meet Sheriff Montgomery of West Memphis, Arkansas, had finally come. I walked down the gravel path and right to the steps of my camper. I was ready for our introduction.

SIXTEEN

He was not near his car, but rather had gone down to the riverbank. I watched him as he stood at the broken railings. He was with Deputy Fisk and they seemed to be studying the current or the flow of the Mississippi. They didn't notice me as I walked up to my camper.

I went over close to where they were standing and sat at the picnic table near my trailer and waited. It was the young deputy who finally saw that I was there. He touched the sheriff on the arm, they turned toward me, and then the two of them came over.

As they walked in my direction, I immediately thought of my father, Captain Morris Burns, a thirty-year veteran with the Rocky Mount Police Department. I wondered how much the sheriff from West Memphis, Arkansas, was going to remind me of the man in whose house I grew up.

"Are you Rose Franklin?" the lawman asked. He was dressed

in uniform, but was not nearly as polished as his junior officer. He was short and square, red-faced, and he stood in front of me with his legs parted and his arms folded across his chest. He waited for my answer.

"Yes," I replied, thinking that both he and my father bore similarities. And I wondered if this man had lost himself, as my father had, to the endless days of governing the dark side of life.

I was not old enough or wise enough to recognize how or when it started with Captain Burns; but I certainly grew to understand the consequences of a man losing his innocence, the way he begins to notice the bad in people before the good. The way the world suddenly turns into something he no longer trusts or approves.

I don't think I was around early enough to pay attention to the details to my father's descent into low opinions and cruel cynicism, but I always somehow suspected that it was intricately connected to his job. I knew that his work was bigger than who he was, more powerful than his personality or his own levelheadedness.

I watched as the sheriff stood sizing me up and wondered if he had become his job or whether his job had become him. I had seen my father and the other men on the force and the way they narrowed their glances in my direction. The immediate judgment of good or evil, mostly evil, the intensity of the eyes, the rigid holding of the jaw, the ability to stand so perfectly still, just like the man was standing in front of me, readying himself for trouble.

The deputy stopped behind him near the tree.

"Are you sure you're Rose Franklin?" the sheriff asked with a smirk.

"Yes," I answered again, deciding to stick to my story and to my new name. "I'm sure."

"Isn't there more to your name than that?" He cleared his throat.

"Rose Franklin Burns Griffith," I replied, feeling my pulse quicken and wondering where he had checked out my identification. "I'm taking my mother's name," I reported.

"Well, you might need to get that legal. Because for now, you're known as Rose Griffith."

He stared at me. His sunglasses hung out of his front pocket. His eyes were dark brown.

"Okay," I answered. "And are you going to tell me who you are?" I asked.

"I'm Sheriff Leon Montgomery," he said, spitting the words out like he was sure I already knew.

The deputy turned in my direction and smiled sympathetically. He shook his head, seeming as if he was sorry for what was happening to me. It reminded me of so many looks just like it I had received during my lifetime.

Growing up in my father's house, I grew accustomed to those glances of sympathy from others, my own feelings of shame. I grew accustomed to wearing the veil of disappointment when it came to my father's parenting skills. And with so many years of embarrassment because of his absences at those events where I wanted him present—events such as recitals, birthday parties, graduation—and even more years feeling the humiliation of his presence during times when I wished him dead—date nights, slumber party nights, after he had been drinking—I finally began spending less and less time at home and more and more time trying to be anywhere that I thought he wouldn't be.

It never seemed to matter, though, because he always knew where to find me, always knew which house, which party, which friend. And there he would show up, yelling and intimidating anybody and everybody around, pulling me out to the car and throwing me in it like some criminal he was picking up.

Trying to get away from my father was the main reason I left home to live with my grandmother every summer from the time I was thirteen, the summer after my mother died. It was the main reason I went to school five hours away instead of studying nursing at the community college close by, and the main reason I married Rip before I turned twenty.

The hold that Captain Morris Burns had over me was broad and heavy. I'm not sure I ever learned how to slide out from under it. Even after he had his first stroke, drooling like a child, falling down, paralyzed, even then he yelled at me for not being respectful, raised his good hand at me as if he intended to strike me because I answered him without saying, "sir." Even then he made me think he was bigger than God.

Even after I was married, grown, and living in my own house, even when I told him I was through with him, never wanted to see him, even then he would call me and as soon as I recognized that it was him on the phone, my hands would start to shake and my voice would change, seem small and faraway.

Even the last day I saw him, that afternoon I visited him in the nursing home, before leaving Rocky Mount, even then he was more than me, took up the whole room, even then I stood beside his bed and felt like a child.

I stared at Sheriff Montgomery and knew that my father, Captain Morris Burns, was not just a man, not just a policeman. He was the whole force wrapped up in himself. And as I steadied myself to have a conversation with this lawman, I knew that for me he was more than just an officer asking me questions. He represented a lifetime of pain and heartache.

"Is there some trouble because of what I'm calling myself, Sheriff Montgomery?" I asked, trying to let go of some of my anger. He was, after all, I told myself, not my father.

"Well." He sucked his teeth. "I wouldn't say trouble."

He walked closer to the table. "I'd just say maybe interest," he said, as he put one leg on the bench where I was sitting. "I'd say there's interest because of what you're calling yourself."

"Uh-huh," I replied. "And who would be interested in that?" I asked.

"Me," he answered. "Maybe your husband in Rocky Mount." He rested his elbow on his knee and dropped his chin in his hand.

"Ex-husband," I said. "He's an ex-husband, and I don't really think he cares what I'm calling myself."

"Well, see, that's where you're wrong. Seems as if he does care." The sheriff had a line of sweat across his brow.

"He says that he's paying the credit bill for a Visa for a Rose Griffith."

He slid his fingers down his chin. "He doesn't know anybody named Rose Franklin. And he doesn't intend paying the bill for somebody other than his wife."

He dropped his leg and stood up next to me. "Excuse me, ex-wife."

I shrugged my shoulders. "I don't see how this is a problem for the West Memphis Sheriff's office," I said, and I clasped my hands in front of me on the table.

"But I tell you what, I will call my ex-husband this afternoon and straighten this all up."

I smiled at him. "Is there something else that you need to ask me about?" I knew if he was anything like my father, he wasn't through with me yet.

He twisted around and looked at the river and then turned back in my direction. I could tell that he tried carrying himself bigger than how he was, but in truth, he wasn't much taller than I am.

"As a matter of fact," he replied. "I do have a few more questions for you."

I waited.

"I'm very interested in why you seem to be showing up asking everybody about my investigation," he said, wiping his forehead with the back of his hand.

"You got some special reason as to why you're so curious about a drowning in a place you claim only to be passing through? Some reason as to why you picked Shady Grove Campground?"

I studied him. He was a spitting image of Captain Burns

when he was interrogating someone. He was cocky and bullish and intimidating, but I wasn't thrown by his tactics.

"Maybe you know something the rest of us don't know," he continued. "Maybe you'd like to let us in on what you're doing here, how it happens that you show up the day we find a missing body, why it is you've decided all of a sudden to take the deceased's last name, how it is you're so familiar with the likes of Lucas and Rhonda Boyd, folks with a known criminal history."

I glanced over to the young deputy. He seemed to grow more and more uncomfortable with the manner in which his boss was talking to me. He shifted in his stance and then squatted on the ground and began pulling at the blades of grass.

"I don't really see why it's any business of yours why I'm staying at this particular campground and why I'm asking questions about a mysterious death. And I don't really think I have to explain to you why I'm calling myself anything. Last time I checked there wasn't any law about the names we choose for ourselves."

He snorted. "Oh, we got some laws all right. Comes under the heading of misrepresentation. Maybe you've heard it called fraud."

He ran his fingers across his salt-and-pepper hair that he had slicked down on the side of his head.

"But let me just move on." He threw his leg back on the seat again and leaned into it.

"You see, it appears suspicious to me that on the day we find a dead man, a dead man without an immediate family except an aged blind mother, a dead man who owns quite a bit of property and a lucrative business, that a woman from North Carolina suddenly shows up out of nowhere and starts asking a lot of questions and then just up and decides to change her name, implying that she's somehow related to the deceased."

Suddenly, his line of thinking was making complete sense.

"You think I'm trying to benefit from Mr. Franklin's death?" I asked, finally understanding what the sheriff was getting at.

"I don't know. You tell me," he answered. Then he angled himself so that he was right beside me, looking over me.

"Why did you go to the coroner's office this morning wanting to know if the cause of death was really suicide? Why are you so suddenly intimate with the Boyds, with Mr. Sawyer? Why did you go to the dead man's house? Ms. Eulene didn't know of any Rose Franklin who was related to the family."

The irony of the situation made me smile. While I was investigating him, he was trying to find out about me.

He assumed I had come into town to lay claim to some of the dead man's property. He thought that I was trying to find out if the death could be listed as something other than suicide so that I could name myself as family and might be entitled to some insurance money.

"Look," I said, using an easier tone for I realized that my arrival in West Memphis and my interest in Lawrence's death could raise a few eyebrows.

"I'm not interested in the Franklin money or any settlement." I relaxed. "I just met Lucas and Rhonda Boyd and Tom Sawyer," I added, though I did not think it was any of his business to ask me about those relationships.

"I just want to know what happened to the man. I just want to make sure he's not written off as some suicide without the case being clearly investigated."

The sheriff eyed me suspiciously. I could tell he didn't believe me. I waited before he responded.

"Well, you don't need to worry your pretty head about this investigation. I'm handling it personally. Mr. Franklin and I had a lot in common and I want to make sure I understand what happened to him, too."

His patronizing words stung. I fought back.

"Like the land here on the river?" I asked.

He dropped his leg and stood very near.

"What?" he asked. I could see how seriously he had taken my question.

"Like the land here on the river," I repeated.

"Didn't you and your brother try to buy this land from Lucas and he wouldn't sell? And didn't Lawrence uncover something of interest somewhere close by? Is that what you meant by having things in common with Mr. Franklin?"

The sheriff pulled in his upper lip, dragging it slowly under his teeth. He took in a deep breath and stood up straight. A voice on the radio suddenly came on calling the sheriff's name.

He turned toward his deputy and pointed with his chin to the car. Deputy Fisk walked by me. We both watched him as he opened the door and sat down on the front seat and answered the call. I turned back to face the sheriff.

"I don't know what it is that you think you know, Miss Franklin," he said, accenting the words *Miss* and *Franklin.* "But my real-estate interests have nothing to do with this man's death and I'm offended at your implication." He put both hands on the table, leaning right beside my face.

"Now I understand from Jimmy Novack that your car will be ready in the morning. Since it seems that you have no further business in West Memphis, then I presume you'll be going on with your trip out west."

I pulled away from him.

"I'm not sure," I said. "Shady Grove does have some lovely people here and I may just stay a few more days.

"There's no reason why I can't, is there?" I asked.

He dropped away from me and then stood up. He glanced over to his deputy, who was looking at us. Fisk raised his chin and starting walking over. The sheriff seemed to take it as a sign.

"You just stay out of our business and I'll have no problem with you," he said. Then he started to move toward the car as his deputy stepped closer to me.

"Sheriff," I called to him. He turned around. Deputy Fisk had gotten to my side.

"Why did you send the body to Nashville?"

His brow wrinkled. "What?" he asked gruffly.

"Mr. Franklin's body," I answered. "Why didn't you let the autopsy be done here or in Memphis?"

He walked back over to where I was sitting and I thought for a moment that he might strike me. Deputy Fisk moved closer to us as if he thought the same thing.

"Not that I have any reason that I have to answer you, but I never sent him to Nashville for the autopsy. That was the hospital's doing." He stood in front of me, blocking the sun.

I was confused.

"Sheriff, you need to get that call," Deputy Fisk said, standing behind me.

"I suppose I'll be able to find you here if I have any more questions?" The sheriff asked.

I nodded slowly.

"Then you have yourself a nice afternoon," he said as he turned and walked to the car. He sat in the driver's side and picked up the receiver.

"He's just showing off," Deputy Fisk said as he moved around to face me. "You can stay as long as you want." And he smiled and nodded and then walked over to the car.

In a few minutes, he got in on the passenger's side, the sheriff started up the car and they drove away. The deputy waved as they exited.

I watched them leave and wondered why Sheriff Montgomery would lie about the autopsy. I was sure that the coroner had said that it was the sheriff who had made that request to take the body to Nashville.

The vehicle exited out the driveway and the campground was once again quiet. I left the picnic table and walked inside my camper. I only had a few hours before I was going back to the hospital to sit with Ms. Lou Ellen. I was already looking forward to a long afternoon nap.

SEVENTEEN

The long nap was not in my cards for that afternoon. When I walked into my camper, my cell phone was ringing. I had forgotten that I had charged it up and turned it on. I noticed the caller's number as I flipped it open.

"Hello," I said, knowing before I spoke that it was Rip.

"Rose? Is that you?"

The sheriff hadn't been bluffing, he had contacted my ex-husband about me being in West Memphis.

"Hey, Rip, how ya doing?"

"How am I doing? I'm doing fine. How are you doing?" he asked, and then added, "Or rather, what are you doing in Tennessee?"

"Arkansas," I replied. "I'm in West Memphis, Arkansas."

"Oh," he responded. "I thought West Memphis was in Tennessee."

There was a pause on the other end. I felt myself smile. Rip never was very good with geography.

"Well, it doesn't matter. I thought you were going to California."

"Arizona," I said. "I was planning to get to Arizona."

"Oh."

"The Bronco broke down. I had to stay here to get it fixed," I explained.

"What's wrong with it?" he asked as if we were still married, as if he was still involved in my car maintenance, as if it mattered to him.

"I don't know. The guy had to order a part."

"What kind of part?" Once a husband always a husband, just maybe not to the same wife.

"I don't know, Rip." I blew out a short breath. "What did you call for?" I asked.

"Because the sheriff called me asking a lot of questions. Said you were staying at a place where known criminals stay, that you were impersonating a family member of some dead man. He wanted to know what you were doing there and if I was authorizing the use of our credit card to a Rose Franklin."

I could hear someone talking in the background. It sounded like he was at a party or some sort of gathering.

"Rose, who's Rose Franklin?"

I waited for a minute, trying to think of how to explain, trying to understand why I felt so light-headed hearing his voice again.

"Rose, you there?" he asked.

I figured he was at the country club. It was Wednesday and

he always golfed on Wednesday afternoons. He had been playing with the same three guys for eighteen years. Even though we
never had much money, Rip had managed a club membership.
It was very important to him to belong.

"You on the course?" I asked.

"Nah, we already finished. I'm just having a drink at the pool."

Then I realized that he was with her. He never liked the pool,
but she did. Her long brown legs, a perfect golden tan; I knew
the first time I saw her that she was the lying-by-the-pool kind
of woman.

"Look, just take the credit card bills to my brother. I'll send
him the money. Just let me get settled and then I'll get my own
card." I heard splashing and a woman laughing.

"Jesus," he said, talking to somebody else, "You just got me
all wet."

"Rip," I said, "Is that all right? Just send the bills to John."

"Okay?" I asked again.

"Yeah, all right." He sounded angry. "Hang on a minute."

I think he was walking away from the commotion.

"You okay, Rose?" he asked. "I mean, you changing your
name and everything. You okay?"

I was touched by his concern.

"Yeah, Rip, I'm fine," I said.

"Well, look, call me if you need me," he replied. Then I heard
him sigh. "And don't worry about the Visa bill. You can pay me
back when you get to California."

"Ari—" I started to say Arizona, but then stopped. I knew it
didn't matter.

I could see him all red-faced from too much sun, his brown hair turning blond, the small white lines around his eyes.

"Okay," he said quickly, as if he was being rushed off the phone. "I'll talk to you later."

And he hung up.

Marriage isn't made or lost in a day, a week, even three months. Not even when there's infidelity or gross disappointment. You can't just "cut your losses and run," as a nurse said when she found out what happened between me and Rip. It isn't that simple or that easy.

Even in the worse situations, the most flagrant examples of unreasonable expectations or no expectations for a marriage, you can't tell me that brides and grooms don't feel something in that ceremony. Two people can't say those vows out loud, in the company of such optimism and hopefulness that is always present at weddings, and not want the best for that relationship, not desire for good things.

You don't just walk away, even in hurt or anger, and not have a few memories of tenderness, a few treasured moments of love. It just isn't possible. And to hear Rip's voice again, even a voice that was now answering to someone else's calls, fulfilling someone else's dreams, took me back twenty years when I said, "I do," and meant it.

You don't live with a man for all of your adult life and not feel a twinge of regret or disappointment when a cell phone rings and you realize that shared life, like the hopes on a wedding day, are gone forever. You just don't get over love that easily.

With the unanticipated phone call and the unforeseen heaviness of heart that followed as its consequence, I knew a nap was out of the question and decided instead to walk again that new path of desire that edged a river and past through mounds of rock. I was going back to Tom Sawyer's.

Another warm and sticky day on the Mississippi; I was already sweating. The low clouds dragged across the sky without any promise of rain while the sun burned white-hot. I changed my clothes to a clean pair of shorts and a T-shirt, since I was still wearing what I had on the previous day. This was the first time I had been in my camper since I had left the riverbank the night before. I took a quick shower, dried and fixed my hair, put on a little makeup, and headed in the direction I had memorized after having only made one trip.

I noticed that the Millers had not returned to their camping site. I figured it would be later that evening or not until the morning before Clara would be released from the hospital. The marrow donation is not a very risky procedure, but doctors usually prefer to watch the donor closely before sending them home. With the added complication of her sister's death, I assumed they'd choose to keep the little girl and allow the parents to stay the night.

I walked past their camper, trying to imagine how difficult their journey had been, how difficult their journey was going to be; I realized that I didn't know which was harder, never being able to know the love of a child or knowing it and then having to let it go.

I headed past the campground and beyond the pond where I first met Tom when he was fishing. I moved past the narrow pier and then remembered the small light I had seen somewhere near there on my first night at Shady Grove. Since it was in the middle of the afternoon and I was in no hurry, I walked to the other side of the small body of water to see what I might find.

Somebody had been there, that was evident. A lawn chair was just at the edge of the surrounding woods. There was a bucket as if someone had been fishing and a large coffee can filled with the butts of long, hand-rolled cigarettes. There were a couple of empty beer cans, a plastic soda bottle, and a fishing tackle box. A pair of old binoculars hung on the back of the chair.

I looked around to see if anyone was nearby, but I didn't see a soul. I noticed several paths going into the woods, but since I wasn't wearing long pants or insect repellent, I just decided to return to the path to Tom's trailer, maybe get him to come back with me later.

I walked around the quarry and saw a bulldozer standing idle near some rocks and a fresh mound of gravel. Because of the tall fence, I couldn't see what else was in the boundaries of the quarry, but I did make note of the white sand both in the mounds that had been dug up and along the edge of the wire fence.

I walked more quickly to Tom's, thinking that he would be interested in what had occurred during my recent visit from the sheriff. When I arrived at his front porch, I realized that his bike was gone. I called out his name and then went on inside to wait for him.

"Hey, you here?" I asked, even though I was sure that he wasn't.

I didn't know how he would feel about me roaming around his place without him there, but I had remembered that I had left my jewelry by the bathroom sink, and I knew I would forget my crystal earrings if I didn't retrieve them while I was thinking about them.

I stood in his den and looked around. I remembered the ease with which we had spent that morning, the way he buttered my toast with long, heavy strokes, the way he smiled as he poured my coffee, laughing that I drank a full cup before speaking two words.

I thought about the way we had made love, how clumsy I felt at first, but then how uncomplicated it became once I saw the look in his eyes, that look of pure gentleness, and once I felt his fingers slide across the back of my neck. After that and the tender kiss we shared, it was as easy as our introduction.

I walked through the kitchen and into the bedroom, heading for the bathroom and my forgotten jewelry, when I glanced over at the nightstand and remembered the passage he had read to me from Thoreau. I walked over and picked up the book, thinking I'd like to see what it was he was reading.

As I opened it to the dog-eared page he had read to me earlier, a small plastic sleeve fell out from between the pages. I bent down to pick it up and I noticed that it was a gold coin, no larger than a quarter, but thicker as if it bore the weight of a nickel.

It was old, faded, but I could still make out that on one side there was a large mountain printed on it with the words *Pike's Peak Gold*. The word *twenty* was printed underneath the stamped picture. On the other side there was a profile of a person with stars around the head and the year, 1860, near the bottom.

I held it up to the window, studying it, wondering about it. It took me a minute, but then I realized what it was. And without completely understanding what I was holding in my hand, I thought of the story he had told me and then immediately decided that Tom must have found some of Percy Dalton's gold.

He knew more about the legend of the slave's Denver gold than he told. He even had one of the coins himself, a coin that Ms. Eulene had said that most of the African-Americans from West Memphis wouldn't have been interested in. "Meant to buy their flesh," she had said, and a chill ran down my spine.

I couldn't believe it. I sat down on the bed, letting the questions fill my head. I sat trying to piece together the things that I knew, trying to find connections between this gold coin, Lawrence's death, and all of Tom's stories.

It was then that I remembered that Tom had mentioned, and Ms. Eulene had said, that Tom and Lawrence were working on the burial ground project together and that Lawrence had made a discovery about the burial ground fairly recently. Surely, the discovery and Mr. Franklin's death had to be related. And if those two things were related then finding this coin was connected to these events as well.

Suddenly, I couldn't help but feel as if something was not

right about this man I had fallen in love with, that something was not right about him and his place on the banks of the Mississippi River. I thought about how little I really knew about the man, how Mary had said he had lived a hard life, had very difficult financial troubles, how he himself mentioned his history of addiction.

I heard the front door open and close. I jumped up from the bed and stuck the coin in my pocket. I walked immediately to the door of the bedroom.

"Hey, there," I called out, trying not to sound nervous or suspicious.

"Hey." He smiled and walked over to me. He dropped a large brown envelope on the counter and then threw his arms around me. He looked like he had heard great news.

"I'm surprised to see you," he said. "I thought you were going to try and rest this afternoon."

I pulled away gently and walked over to the kitchen table.

"Yeah, I was, but the sheriff unnerved me with his visit." I took a seat.

"Get this." I was trying to sound normal, unaffected by recently acquired news. I acted as normally as I could. "He thinks I came into town and took Lawrence Franklin's name so that I might get some money from his estate." I rolled my eyes and threw up my hands. "Can you believe that?"

Tom raised his eyebrows and stepped toward the refrigerator. "Want something cold to drink?" he asked. He didn't sound at all concerned that I had been there without him.

"No, I'm fine," I answered.

He took out a soda and popped the top. Then he sat down next to me.

"That's something," he replied. "Did he give you a hard time?" he asked.

"He tried," I said, "but he didn't really bother me. The deputy seemed embarrassed for me."

I could feel my heart thumping. I took a few deep breaths to try and calm down.

"He's just a big bag of wind," Tom responded as he took a swallow of his drink.

"Well, I don't think he cares too much for me," I said.

"Yeah?" Tom smiled. "You make him mad?" he asked.

I laughed a bit. "I just didn't make things easy for him is all," I answered.

"Well, good for you," he said. He took another long swallow.

"So, what are you planning to do now?" he asked, setting the can on the table. "I have a wonderful story." He reached over and took one of my hands.

He seemed so loving, so truthful, so innocent. I was a whirl of emotions.

"I thought I'd go on to the hospital early," I said, trying to create an easy exit for myself, not paying any attention to his mention of a story. "I figure Rhonda could use a little help with Ms. Lou Ellen's dinner; and besides she's been there all day." I stood up from the table.

He stood up, too. "Let me just take a quick shower," he said, "and I'll drive you over."

"No, no," I protested. "I'll get Lucas to take me to Memphis.

I'm sure he was planning to go back anyway. Maybe he and Rhonda might want to get a bite to eat somewhere together," I added, thinking my idea sounded very believable.

"Okay, then," he said, and pulled me into himself. "Will I see you in the morning?" he asked.

"Of course," I answered and then slowly backed away, stepping over to the door.

"Rose," he said softly, reaching over and taking my hand in his. "Are you okay?"

I smiled as genuinely as I could. "I'm just fine," I said and opened the door. I stood on the porch. "I'll call you tonight from the hospital," I added as I closed the door.

I hurried up the path before he could answer, knowing that I didn't have his phone number and that I had completely forgotten to get my jewelry. I reached in my pocket and pressed the coin against my leg.

EIGHTEEN

I went first to my camper and grabbed a few things to take with me to the hospital. I knew that I would be there a long time, so I took a sweatshirt and a pair of sweatpants, my toothbrush, a few other toiletries, and a magazine. Then I saw my cell phone and I don't know why, but I sat down at the table and I pressed the key that listed the last caller's number. Then I hit Send. It was just habit causing me to want to speak again to Rip.

"Yeah," he said quickly, without realizing it was my number on his screen. "Honey, I got it," he said to someone else, to her.

I hit the button marked End and then turned my phone off. I should have known better than to think I could tell him about Tom and the gold, about Shady Grove. He would have never understood. And even if I wasn't completely over him, I knew I could no longer rely on him to render a concerned and informed decision about how to live my life; I could no longer call him for support.

I walked over to the office and found Lucas. He was helping Mary with the paperwork. He said that he was more than happy to drive me back to Baptist Hospital. He was anxious to check on Rhonda and his mother-in-law and anxious, Mary added, to get away from the office. I helped take inventory of all the food Mrs. Franklin had sent over. Mary wanted to make sure we didn't lose any containers and was thinking that a campground covered-dish dinner might be a nice way for us to show our concern for the Miller family. We were both sure that they would be leaving for Kentucky soon.

Lucas walked over to his trailer and then pulled around the truck. He honked the horn and I joined him. We took off down the driveway and out of the campground. I rolled down the window and stuck out my arm.

"So, little sister, did you get any rest?" he asked.

I shook my head. "No, but it's okay. I'm sure I'll get to sleep a couple of hours tonight," I said.

He nodded and turned the knob on his radio. He found a country station.

"So, you and Thomas?" he asked, not completely finishing the question, but making very clear what it was that he was fishing for.

I realized that news traveled faster at Shady Grove than it did at the hospital where I had worked. We turned onto the paved road, past the railroad tracks, and beside the oil tanks.

I smiled. "I don't know," I said.

"Tom's a good man," he said, driving ahead and then stopping at the intersection and looking in both directions before traveling on.

"So I've heard," I replied, remembering those exact words that Mary had used earlier that day.

He hummed to the song on the radio. I felt awkward having the conversation, especially knowing what I had just learned. I felt for the coin. It was still in my pocket.

"There's nobody I trust more than Thomas Sawyer," he said, causing me to wonder about his marriage and why he would trust someone more than his wife.

As if he could read my mind, he added, "Rhonda feels the same way."

I nodded without a reply.

"How long have the two of you known each other?" I asked, thinking maybe he could shed some light on the man I thought I loved.

"We served in Vietnam together," Lucas replied. "We went on the same day and signed up for duty." He merged into the traffic going over the bridge.

"We both knew we were getting in over our heads." He waved at the car behind him.

"Anyway," he said, as if he didn't care sorting through those days, as if there was pain in those memories, "Thomas has been a good friend to me and Rhonda."

I didn't say anything. I just wondered what Lucas knew about Tom's relationship with Lawrence, what he knew about his interest and acquisition of the gold coin, if perhaps the three of them, Lucas, Rhonda, and Thomas were in this together.

"Who owns the quarry next to the campground?" I asked, quickly changing the subject, remembering seeing it as I walked over to Thomas's from the campground. I was curious about the property.

"I do," he answered. "But I lease it to the Kunar family. They had the quarry there before I bought the land to develop into Shady Grove, so I just let them keep the property, pay me a little rent every year. I get my gravel free."

I turned to see the river flowing behind us. There were a couple of barges coming toward Tennessee. The bridge took us farther away from the campground.

"Thomas own his land?" I asked.

Lucas shook his head. "No." Then he glanced over to me.

"Why all this interest in land ownership, little sister?" he asked.

I smiled. "Just wondering is all." Then I added, "I mean, I just was curious why Tom never bought his own property."

"It's not for lack of opportunity," Lucas said with a laugh. "I offered to give it to him when I bought Shady Grove," he added.

I was surprised. "Why did you do that?" I asked.

"Because it's like I told you, there's nobody I'd trust more than that man, and besides it was him who helped me get the property."

"Oh?" I replied, now very interested.

The breeze felt good, so I angled myself against the door so that my head and shoulders were mostly out the window.

"Tom cosigned with Ms. Lou Ellen for Shady Grove. I'd never have been able to get the loan without his help."

There wasn't much traffic on the interstate and we enjoyed a leisurely pace.

"Having just gotten out of prison and with a fairly long record at the county courthouse; let's just say the banks were not interested in backing my real-estate ventures."

We exited off the interstate and headed into downtown Memphis.

"Lucas, were Tom and Lawrence Franklin close friends?" I asked. I knew what Tom had said and what Ms. Eulene had said, now I just wanted another opinion.

We stopped at the light.

"Tom's friendly with mostly everyone," he answered. "Most everybody who knows him considers him a friend." He seemed to be thinking about the question.

"But close friends?" He turned in the direction of the hospital. "I don't think Tom gets very close to people," he said.

I wondered what this meant.

"Yeah, but you say you trust him completely," I replied. "How can you trust somebody that doesn't let people get close to them?"

We headed around the back of the hospital toward the visitor's parking garage.

"Trusting somebody isn't always about being close to them," he answered as he looked around trying to find the entrance.

"When you really trust a person you don't have to be intimate with them," he added, then continued as he found the right direction to take, "Thomas Sawyer has already proven himself to me more times than I can count. I don't need to be with him all the time to know the kind of man he is."

He pulled into the garage, stopped, rolled down his window, and pulled a ticket out of the meter.

"To answer your question though, I do know that Thomas cared about Lawrence. They had grown up together, gone to school together. Sure, they were friends, and they were working on some historical project."

"Yeah?" I asked, trying to find out what Lucas knew. "What was that about?" I asked as we pulled into a parking space.

"Mr. Franklin was looking for some burial site," he answered, repeating the same story I had now heard from three people.

"Thomas was helping him." He got out of his side and we walked around the truck.

"They ever find what they were searching for?" I asked, already knowing the answer.

"I don't know, little sister," he replied. "I don't know what anybody is really searching for," he added, looking at me with a suspicious eye.

I let his statement pass without a reply.

"I do know that Thomas Sawyer is a fine and upstanding man, and if he's your choice for a beau, then you couldn't have found a nicer person."

He opened the glass door that led to the stairwell. I walked through and we headed down to the second floor where we entered the hospital lobby and made our way to the elevator. We rode two floors up without any further conversation.

The door was closed, so we knocked first and then we walked into the room and found Rhonda painting Ms. Lou Ellen's toenails. At first, Rhonda spun around, trying to cover up what she was doing. When she saw it was us, she blew out a breath and continued her task.

They had chosen a very bright red polish. The patient was sitting up slightly in the bed, but was still fairly groggy from her recent operation.

"She said they had to be done now." Rhonda rolled her eyes at us. "They took off what she had on before they did surgery."

She was almost finished. Two toes were left.

"I've had my nails painted every summer for more than fifty years," Ms. Lou Ellen said with a drowsy Southern accent. "I'm not about to stop having them polished now just because my hip is out of joint."

"I suppose the nurses don't know about this," I said, quite sure that they were the ones who removed the polish to start with. With surgery, the color of toenails can provide important information about blood circulation.

"No, they don't know about it," Rhonda said in exasperation. "I've had to sneak the polish in and now sneak it on. Honestly, I haven't been this deceptive since I was dropping acid."

Lucas laughed. "Oh, little sister," he even called his wife by that name. He went over and hugged her.

"Be careful, Lucas Boyd!" The shout came from the patient.

He stepped back in fear that he had somehow wounded the older woman.

"She's terrible at this already. If you start getting in her way, I'll have Spurned Cherry all over my bed."

I laughed and moved carefully over to the chair by the patient's side. I set my bag beside the bedside table and sat down. Lucas eased over next to me, carefully so as not to shake the bed or unsettle his wife.

"Ya'll are here early," Rhonda said as she finished the last toe.

Ms. Lou Ellen closed her eyes.

"I figured you had been here long enough," I whispered. "Besides, I didn't have anything else to do this afternoon."

Rhonda put the tiny brush back in the bottle and twisted it shut. Then she reached over and grabbed a magazine and began fanning her mother's feet.

I checked the patient's IV bag and her lines. Everything looked fine.

"How's the care here?" I asked.

"They've been real good," she answered. "I've just now been able to get these toes done because somebody has come in every fifteen or twenty minutes." She kept fanning. Then she stopped and blew on them.

"Did you go to St. Jude's?" Rhonda asked me. She knew that was where I was heading when I left that morning.

I nodded.

"It's not good?" she asked as if she had already heard the news.

I shook my head. "Jolie died this morning."

"Lord, bless 'em," Lucas said, and he and Rhonda bowed their heads.

"Amen," Lucas said after a few minutes.

Rhonda jerked her head up and started fanning again.

"Amen," Ms. Lou Ellen said, and then fell back to sleep.

"We'll need to do something for that nice family, Lou," Rhonda said, speaking to her husband.

He nodded.

"There's already a ton of food that Ms. Eulene Franklin gave us when she heard."

"How did she hear?" Rhonda asked. She touched the shiny red nail of her mother's big toe.

"I told her," I said. "I went over to meet Ms. Eulene after I was at the hospital."

Rhonda nodded. She pulled the sheet over her mother's feet.

A nursing assistant walked in about that time with a tray of food. She sniffed the air.

"Is that nail polish I smell?" she asked.

Rhonda shook her head innocently. "I think it's the cleaning fluid," she said.

She made a huffing noise. "They use the smelliest stuff," the attendant reported, and then walked out the door, closing it behind her.

Rhonda raised her eyebrows at me and I laughed. I noticed the clock, thinking that four thirty was fairly early for dinner, but then I realized that the patient probably hadn't had anything to eat all day.

Rhonda lifted the cover on the tray. It was broth and Jell-O and a small cup of ice. She put down the cover, deciding it wasn't worth waking her mother for.

We sat for about an hour and talked about the surgery and the prognosis and then I noticed Rhonda yawn and look at her watch. I could tell that she was tired.

"Look, Rhonda, you've been here all day. You and Lucas go ahead," I said. "I brought my stuff and I'm going to stay until the morning like I told you," I added.

Rhonda seemed reluctant to leave.

"Have you had dinner, little sister?" Lucas asked.

I shook my head. "I had lunch at the Franklins'."

The couple smiled knowingly.

"You won't be hungry then until midnight," Rhonda said. Then she glanced around the room. "You sure about staying?" She peered at me.

I nodded.

"This seems like too much to ask. You already came this morning." She shook her head. "This is just so nice of you," she said, gathering up her things and giving them to Lucas.

"Thank you for today." She pulled me up from my seat in a big hug.

I recovered my breath and remained standing next to the bed.

"You're welcome," I said, worried that she would hug me again.

"Little sister," Lucas said, "this means a lot to our family."

Then I worried that he was going to hug me, too. But he didn't. He just threw one arm around me. It was still a crushing move.

"You make sure and call us if you need us." He pulled his arm away and winked at me.

"We'll be fine," I answered, glancing over to her mother. Ms. Lou Ellen was sleeping soundly.

"I'll be back first thing in the morning," Rhonda said.

Then she went over and kissed her mother on the cheek.

She paused. "I don't know," she said. "Maybe I should stay."

"Look, I'm used to third shift and you're going to need your rest for when she comes home. It's fine. This is what I do," I said.

Rhonda sighed and moved away from the bed. The two of them walked out the door, stepping backward. I walked with them and held open the door.

"Really, thank you," Rhonda said again.

I nodded. "Okay." I closed the door behind them.

I checked again the IV lines and the position of the pillows in the bed. I pulled up the sheet and assessed the condition of the bandage. Everything looked fine. I fluffed the sheet around the patient and walked around the bed to sit down beside her. I was glad to have some quiet time to think about everything that had happened that day.

I reached into my pocket and pulled out the gold coin. I held it up to the light and studied it again. I thought that Thomas might have already realized that it was stolen, and that I might find myself in bigger trouble with the sheriff than I was already in.

Impersonating the family member of a dead person and stealing from a man that I slept with the first night I met him, I was racking up both moral and criminal offenses, and I hadn't even been away from North Carolina for more than a couple of days. I slipped the coin back in my pocket and stared out the window. I decided to name first the things I did know.

Lawrence Franklin was extremely interested in finding an old burial ground that was used by his ancestor to bury the bodies of some drowned slaves. He had asked for help from Tom and the city manager. Apparently, he had recently discovered the general area that he thought was the historical site. There was a red grave marker in his jacket pocket.

He had revealed his findings to his mother, his neighbors, the quarry manager, Tom, the Boyds, and the sheriff. On the day before he was leaving town, he had discovered another important clue, on the day he was planning an early business trip to St. Louis, he disappeared.

A little girl saw him down by the banks of the Mississippi at the campground sometime after he left his house. And three days after he was declared missing by his mother, they found his body only a few hundred yards from Shady Grove. It was initially ruled as drowning by suicide.

Evidence of drowning was established, but white sand, not native to the Mississippi River, was found in his airways. A complete autopsy had not yet been rendered. That was what I knew about Mr. Lawrence Franklin.

The Boyds were a mysterious couple who had served time in prison, owned a campground, and cavorted with ex-criminals. They appeared to have cleaned up their lives, found Jesus, but they had no other known means of income except the campground and they seemed to spend a lot of time boating up and down the river.

Tom Sawyer was a fisherman who knew a lot about history and geography. He knew the stories of buried gold and of a possible burial site. He lived near the campground and was friends with the deceased and with the Boyds. He was an alcoholic, a veteran, owned no property except his trailer. A gold coin, the same kind he said was what the slave had, was found in his possession. That was what I knew about Tom Sawyer.

I looked over to Ms. Lou Ellen. She was moving her lips as if she was holding a very important conversation. I turned back to the window, realizing I knew more.

According to Lucas Boyd, Thomas was an upstanding, trustworthy man. "Thomas Sawyer has proven himself to me more times than I can count," the campground owner had said, without revealing too many details. And yes, he did know Lawrence, but probably not well.

Then there was the sheriff, an obnoxious man who kept showing up in the story. He was there when they pulled up the dead man from the river, had the dead man's jacket taken from the scene, and then gave it to Lawrence's mother. He was at the emergency room when they brought him in. He kept sending his personnel to the campground, trying to find out more information, and he knew that Lawrence had found the burial site. And, most important, I remembered, he had been very motivated to buy the campground with his brother about a year earlier.

I let out a deep breath. Ms. Lou Ellen stirred. She turned her head in my direction. More than several hours had past since her surgery.

"Rose?" she asked. "Is your name Rose?"

I smiled and stood next to the bed.

"Yes, ma'am," I answered. "I met you just yesterday." I knew the surgery and the pain medicine could make a patient disoriented. "At the campground," I added.

She smiled. "I remember you," she said. Then she yanked aside her sheet and looked down at her toes. "Nice," she said, drawing out the word into three, maybe four, syllables. She covered her legs back up. Then she turned to face me again.

"Do you think I might have something to drink?" she asked.

"Absolutely," I answered. I walked around the bed and pulled the table in front of her.

"You have soup and juice and Jell-O," I said, pulling off the cover to the tray.

"Yum-yum," the older woman replied. "How about a little Jell-O?" And she smiled.

"It's green," I said, yanking off the top and picking up the spoon. I took a little and held it to her mouth.

The patient took the spoonful. "Mmmm," she responded, sounding more alert. "Just the same color as money."

I was glad to see she still had her sense of humor intact.

I fed her a few more spoonfuls.

"That's just fine," she said, holding her hand to her mouth. Then she pointed to the cup of ice. "Is there anything in there?" she asked.

"Would you like some soda?" I asked.

"Something clear," she answered. "I feel a little unsettled." She slid her tongue around her lips.

I could tell she felt dry. I reached in my bag and handed her some Chap Stick. She took it and spread it across her lips and handed the tube back to me.

"I'll see what they have," I replied and walked outside to the nurses' station.

An attendant showed me to the snack room and poured me a glass of Sprite to take to Ms. Lou Ellen. That's when I met the nurse on duty, introduced myself, and got the full report about the surgery and the prognosis. Everything seemed to be fine for the older woman.

The nurse, Maria, appeared glad to have me in the room with the patient since the unit was short-staffed that night and she was busy with a couple of people whose surgeries hadn't gone nearly as well as Ms. Lou Ellen's. I assured her that I would be there all night and that I would take good care of her, calling her if I needed assistance.

Maria was young, and I could tell, quite overwhelmed. I walked back to the room, remembering those early days for me at the hospital, the way I got stuck with all the late shifts, all the most needy patients. I was thinking about my youth and was almost at Ms. Lou Ellen's room when I glanced down the hall and noticed the ambulance attendant from earlier in the day, the woman, Becky Kunar.

She pulled out the chart from the holder by the door of a room and was reading it. She was not in her EMT uniform, but rather was dressed in hospital scrubs, blue shirt with blue pants, netting over her hair and her shoes. She looked as if she might be working in the operating room.

I thought that I might speak to her, tell her about how Ms. Lou Ellen was doing, thank her for getting her to the hospital in a timely and professional manner, so I waited for her to walk by. She went into the room and soon came back out wheeling a patient resting in the bed. She was talking to the older man she was transporting when she went past, and I could see that she didn't recognize me. I decided not to interrupt her conversation with the patient.

I walked into the room and Ms. Lou Ellen had pulled herself up a little in the bed. She had opened the drawer on the table and was going through some of her things that Lucas had brought her.

"Is there a comb in here?" she asked.

I smiled. "Well," I answered, moving closer to her, "I don't know."

I put down the drink and found a brush for the older woman. She took it and tried fixing her hair. She gave up after a few strokes. The IV line and the energy it took made it a more difficult task than she had anticipated.

"Would you like some Sprite?" I asked.

She nodded. I leaned down, placing the cup with the straw near her mouth. She took a couple of swallows and relaxed.

"Darling," she said as I placed the cup back on the table and took my seat beside her.

"Yes, ma'am," I answered.

"Getting old is not for sissies."

I smiled. "No, ma'am, I guess it isn't." I reached over and returned the brush to the drawer. "But you aren't getting old," I said, trying to cheer her up.

"Darling, I'm ancient," she replied, "and my bones and joints are telling me so." She winced as she tried to move over.

I stood up, attempting to reposition her pillows.

"Well, maybe you shouldn't listen to them." I slid the sheet back and pulled a pillow underneath her knee. "Listen to something else."

"Honey, you listen to what speaks the loudest and right now, it's a hip bone yelling at me." I draped the sheet back around her, tucking her in.

I sat down. I picked up her hand and stroked her long fingers.

She closed her eyes. "What are you listening to?" she asked.

The question caught me off-guard. "Ma'am?" I replied.

She repeated herself. "What are you listening to, Rose Franklin?"

"I don't know, Ms. Lou Ellen," I answered. "I'm not sure I know."

She nodded and closed her eyes. And as if she could read my troubled thoughts, see the coin I had stolen from Thomas, understand the stories that had confused me, the feelings that surprised me, she squeezed my hand.

"You need to trust somebody, Rose Franklin." She smiled. She took another sip of drink, slid back down in the bed, and nodded off again.

"If only I knew who that should be," I replied, but Ms. Lou Ellen was already fast asleep.

I glanced at the clock on the wall and saw that it was getting late. An announcement was made that visiting hours were over and I settled in for a long night of caregiving.

NINETEEN

Ms. Lou Ellen drifted in and out of sleep as Maria came in a couple of times and checked the patient's vital signs and the dressing. She said that Ms. Lou Ellen would need to get up again—for the second time since she had gotten to the room—sometime before breakfast.

I assured her that I would help her with getting the patient out of the bed and over to the chair. For the rest of the night, we agreed to let her sleep. And with the way the older woman seemed to be snoozing, I didn't think sleeping through the night was going to be a problem. She wasn't showing any signs of pain or discomfort.

Since she was sleeping so soundly, I decided to go to the coffee shop downstairs and get a little something to eat. Rhonda was right. It was midnight and the lunch I had devoured at Mrs. Franklin's had finally worn off. I stopped by the nurses' station and told Maria I was going downstairs and asked if she wanted anything. She kindly refused, saying that she had already taken her dinner break.

I found my way down to the twenty-four-hour coffee shop and ordered a burger and fries. Then I sat down to wait for my order to be prepared. I picked up a newspaper and began reading the day's headlines.

"Well, hello there." A voice came from just beside me.

I looked over, and there was Deputy Fisk, still as polished and ordered as I remembered him from the previous day and earlier that morning.

"Hey," I said, sounding like we were old friends. His appearance surprised me, but I wasn't displeased to see him or alarmed at his presence.

"What are you doing here?" I asked, placing the paper on the table.

"Bar brawl," he reported, pointing with his chin toward the emergency department that was just around the corner.

"I had to bring a guy in for some stitches before I can take him to jail." He was still on duty.

I smiled. "You eating?" I asked.

"I thought I might get a bite," he answered.

I slid the paper over, making room on the table for our dinners. "Well, here, join me," I said.

The man behind the grill called out my order and I excused myself, got up from my seat, went over, and picked it up. I returned and set my tray down and got some extra napkins. By the time I was at the table Fisk had ordered and was sitting across from me. He was drinking a soda.

"What about you?" he asked. "These are late hours for a tourist."

"I'm here with Rhonda Boyd's mother." I took the wrap off of my hamburger.

"Oh, that's right," he replied. "She fell this morning."

I took a bite and felt a bit of surprise that he would have known about the accident.

He could tell what I was thinking.

"Small town," he said. "One channel on the scanner for all emergencies," he explained.

He had heard the call for the ambulance.

The cook yelled out his order and he got up from his seat to retrieve it. He returned and was eating the same meal I was. I smiled.

"Healthy living," I commented.

He laughed. "I'll work it off tomorrow," he said.

We ate a few bites without speaking.

"I'm sorry about Sheriff Montgomery today," he said, wiping off some ketchup that was smeared in the corner of his mouth.

"That's okay," I replied, eating a French fry. "My dad was a big lawman. I'm used to that kind of interview."

He smiled. "Where was your dad working?" he asked.

"Back home," I answered, "North Carolina," I added.

"Oh, that's right," he said, taking another bite, "Rocky Mount."

I nodded, feeling a little disconcerted that he knew my hometown.

His radio went off, but he reached down and turned down the volume.

"I was the one who had to check you out," he said, seeing my surprise.

I nodded, feeling a bit vulnerable. I finished my burger.

"We'll wrap up this case next week," he said. "It'll be ruled as an accidental drowning."

I wiped my mouth and took a couple of swallows from my drink. "What makes you think that?" I asked.

"They'll find no evidence of self-inflicted harm and nobody wants his mother to have to suffer with the grief of thinking her son killed himself. It just isn't important whether he committed suicide or not. And there won't be enough evidence to prove it one way or another."

I nodded, thinking that it was a nice way of going with the story, but then I thought about all the things I had been learning. "Well, maybe not suicide, but what about homicide?" I asked.

He ate his last bite of burger and leaned slightly across the table. "What do you mean?" he asked, appearing very interested in what I had just said. "What makes you ask a question like that?"

I shrugged my shoulders.

He sat waiting for my reply. And I remembered what Ms. Lou Ellen said and decided to trust somebody. And in that second of recollection, I decided to trust him, Deputy J. Fisk.

"Do you know the story of the slave's gold?" I asked, pouring out the rest of my French fries on a napkin.

He shook his head.

"Did you know that Mr. Lawrence Franklin was real interested in the land around the campground, that he thought he had discovered a burial ground for slaves and other folks near there?"

He shook his head again. He sat very still, interested. He stopped chewing.

I wiped off my hands and reached in my pocket and took out Tom's coin. I placed it on the table between us.

"I found this at Tom Sawyer's trailer," I said hesitantly.

"He's the one who told me the story about a slave trying to buy his family with gold coins. He said people were thinking that it was buried somewhere in West Memphis."

Deputy Fisk picked up the coin and examined it.

"Tom was also helping Lawrence look for the burial ground and Mrs. Franklin, Lawrence's mother, said that he had found it."

I took a deep breath as the deputy waited for the rest of my story. He glanced up at me and then again at the coin that he was still holding in his left hand.

"At first I thought it was Sheriff Montgomery who knew about the gold and that it was somewhere near Shady Grove. I heard about his interest in buying the land, but Lucas wouldn't sell it. So, I thought that maybe he was the one who knew the gold was somewhere near the campground and when Lawrence was snooping around, had him killed or something."

The deputy smiled and I assumed that he thought I was being a little dramatic. I figured it was sounding like a script for a television show. I paused. I certainly hoped that I was right to be telling all this to the young deputy.

"But now I think it may be Tom," I finally acknowledged.

"I think he knew where the gold was and that Lawrence knew, too, or that together they found the burial site near Shady Grove and also found the gold. I don't know." I took another swallow from my drink.

"I just know that it's very strange that Tom knew about Lawrence and the burial ground and then also had this gold coin." I looked around, hoping no one was listening to the conversation. I noticed that the cook at the grill was watching us.

"It's all crazy, I know," I said.

The deputy still had not responded. I could tell that he was thinking about what to say, what to do. "Can I keep this?" he asked, referring to the coin.

I thought about it. "I suppose. I stole it this afternoon. My guess is that Tom will realize it sometime soon."

He nodded and unbuttoned his front pocket and dropped the coin in it. I heard the radio dispatcher on his radio calling his name. He lifted his eyebrows. "I guess those stitches are done. I better go."

He took his tray over to the trash can and dumped his trash. He hadn't eaten everything on his plate. Then he walked over to the table and stood right beside me. He laid his hand on my shoulder. "Captain Burns would be proud of you." And he turned and walked out of the room.

As soon as he said my father's name, I felt the air fly out of my lungs.

How did he know his name? I wondered, then thinking that

he must have discovered it when he did the background check on me. Still, something troubled me about the way he had acted, and I wanted to talk to him a little more, find out what he intended to do with my suspicions.

I jumped up, threw my trash away, and followed him to the emergency department. When I rounded the corner into the waiting area he was nowhere to be found.

I glanced around the large lobby. There were a few people sitting on chairs and the sofa, a woman sitting in the registration area. I didn't spot the deputy, so I decided to head back upstairs. As I turned to walk to the elevator I ran smack into Dr. Lehman, the medical examiner I had spoken to earlier that day.

"Hey, watch out!"

But it was too late. I had already plowed right into him, causing him to spill the cup of coffee he was holding. I could tell it was hot and now burning his chest.

"Oh, heavens," I exclaimed. "I'm so sorry." I tried wiping his jacket off with my hand. I was only making things worse.

"Don't worry about it."

He seemed agitated by my attempts to clean him up. He pulled away. He shook the coffee off his hands and could see that some of the papers he was holding were now also stained. He made a huffing noise.

"I'm so sorry. I wasn't watching where I was going."

"Yeah, well, next time just be careful." He wiped some more.

I looked over to where I had just eaten my dinner and I ran over to the grill and grabbed some napkins. I came back and handed them to him. The coroner held his papers up and I took them from him as he tried to clean himself off. Then he finally glanced up at my face and recognized who I was.

"It's you," he said, taking back his folder and handing me the wet napkins.

"Yep," I said with a hint of embarrassment.

"The Franklin family member," he said, naming me.

I nodded. He looked down at his coat again and shook his head.

"Well, I guess I didn't need that coffee anyway." He lifted his face.

"I'm really sorry," I said again. I balled-up the soggy napkins in my hand.

"It's fine." He blew out another breath. "What are you still doing here?" he asked.

"I'm staying with a friend," I answered. "A patient," I explained.

He wiped his papers against his pants leg. "Oh," he said.

"By the way," he added, surprising me that he would still hold a conversation. "I checked out the autopsy in Nashville." He stood up straight and smoothed down the front of his stained jacket.

I was listening.

"They never did it," he said, peering at me with a raised eyebrow. "They said they never had a record for the arrival of a Lawrence Franklin."

I was speechless. I took a few steps away from the doctor, giving him a little more room, waiting to hear more.

"The paramedics ended up finally taking the body to Little Rock, but my friend who works there said the corpse didn't get to the morgue until late that night. That it was almost ten hours after the reported time of finding the body." He glanced at his watch.

"Anyway, it's going to be ruled as an accidental drowning. Mr. Lawrence had a history of heart disease in his family and there was evidence of the left anterior descending artery being partially blocked."

He straightened his jacket. "Since there was no one present at the time of death, no information available about what he was doing on the morning he disappeared, and because of the similarities between drowning and heart failure, they're just closing the books on it, naming it an accident."

I couldn't believe it.

"What about the white sand you saw in his airways?" I asked.

He shook his head. "No presence of any of that when he finally got to the university hospital. His airways were cleaned out." He shrugged.

"Anyway, the weight of his lungs was slightly increased. There was evidence of diatoms native to the Mississippi River, contusions and abrasions that could have occurred postmortem, and no stones or vegetation found in the victim's hands. They're sticking with the closed coronary artery and accidental drowning."

I was relieved for Ms. Eulene because I knew now that she would be able to have her son's funeral at the church instead of at the campground, that she'd be able to acquire any insurance he had put aside for her, and that there would be an end to any more talk and speculation about her son committing suicide. But I also felt disappointment. We would never really be able to understand how Mr. Franklin had died.

"How did his airways get cleaned out?" I asked.

The coroner shook his head.

"Little Rock just assumed I did it on the initial assessment. They aren't making a big deal about it."

He watched me closely. "And I'm not either," he added, and I understood that he could be held liable for not performing and documenting a complete examination when the body first arrived on his shift.

I nodded. I had no reason to get him into trouble. He had been very gracious and kind toward me. But I did wonder what happened to the body during those hours it was supposed to go to Nashville and then got sent to Little Rock.

I thought of one more question for the medical examiner.

"Does anybody else know about the autopsy findings?" I asked, remembering the deputy's earlier statement.

The coroner shook his head again.

"No, I know because I went to school with the head medical examiner over at Little Rock. Our wives are best friends. Anyway, he's very particular about not sharing his report until he's documented it. So, keep a lid on it, would you? I shouldn't have told you any of this."

I understood and respected his request.

"Thank you. And you can trust me." I couldn't explain it at

the time, but I felt somewhat dishonest in having said those words. "I'm sorry about your lab coat," I said again.

He waved off my apology.

"Don't worry about it. It's time for me to go home anyway. I don't need the caffeine." He smiled.

"You take care now and watch where you're going." He headed down the hall.

I threw away the napkins and found my way to the elevator. I felt worse than I had before I came downstairs.

TWENTY

I was on my way to Ms. Lou Ellen's room when I decided to stop by and see Maria, to let her know that I had returned.

"You get something good and greasy?" she asked, smiling when I walked behind the tall desk that wrapped around the nurses' station.

She was sitting in a small cubicle behind a partition, working on charts.

"Hamburger," I answered.

"Mmmmm," she responded. "With fries?"

"There's no other way," I replied.

The elevator opened and we leaned around the corner to see that a nurse was returning with the patient who had left earlier with the ambulance attendant.

"Great." Maria sighed. "Just when I thought I was getting a break."

I knew she meant that she was going to have to help the patient resettle in the room now that the procedure he had just had was completed. She stood up from her seat and stretched.

She threw her hands straight above her head and then dropped at the waist, touching her toes. She turned from side to side. Then she stood up and reached over, grabbing her stethoscope. "You don't want a job, do you?"

I laughed. "Not yet," I answered. "But maybe you could quit this gig and start a yoga group."

She smiled and started to walk out of the station. "More money in cleaning bedpans," she said.

"By the way, your patient is doing very well. I checked on her while you were gone. Ran her vitals, repositioned her. She was alert and oriented and then fell right back to sleep."

She grabbed a chart. "When did her toes get painted?" she asked and looked at me for a response.

I smiled and shrugged my shoulders, trying to act innocent. "I'm glad she's doing well," I said, and then I remembered something that was bothering me.

"Maria, do you know the woman who took that patient down?" I asked, referring to the man that was being wheeled down the hall, that man she had to get resettled. "Her first name is Becky and she runs an ambulance shift?"

"Becky Kunar," the nurse answered as she flipped through a few pages in a chart. "She works a couple of jobs, she's all over the hospital."

She started out the door and appeared to think of something

that might interest me. "She's from over where you're staying, West Memphis. She's engaged to some deputy there."

Kunar, I thought. I suddenly remembered that the other paramedic had mentioned her being engaged to Fisk. I considered her last name and wondered where I had heard Kunar recently. I knew somebody had mentioned that name.

It was almost one o'clock in the morning and I was getting drowsy. I patted my cheeks trying to wake up.

I followed Maria down the hall and stopped at Ms. Lou Ellen's room. I opened the door and then turned, facing it to close it as quietly as I could. When I turned around to see the patient, she was awake and watching me.

"Well, hey there, sleepyhead,"

I moved closer to the bed. The light was on above her.

She smiled. "Did you get some dinner?" she asked.

"I sure did," I answered. "Are you hungry?"

Her face pinched in a knot. "Maybe in the morning," she replied. "I'm still not feeling too ready for food."

She pointed to the chair beside her. "Come sit down and talk to me," she said.

"What did you eat?" she asked.

"Burger and fries," I said.

"No green Jell-O?" she asked.

I moved over to the large reclining chair positioned next to her bed. I stood beside it. "No, I told them to save all the green Jell-O for the patient in room four-fifteen."

She folded her hands across her lap.

"Tell me a story," she said.

"What kind of story?" I asked.

"About you," she replied. "I don't know anything about you," she added.

I turned the chair to face her and sat down. "Okay," I answered, "What would you like to know?"

"I want to know about your kin, about where you come from," she said.

I studied her. "Aren't you sleepy?" I asked, thinking that I didn't really want to share my history at that early hour in the morning.

"You know I've been sleeping all day," she replied. "Stimulate me," she said, shaking her head with a dramatic flair.

I laughed. "My story is hardly stimulating," I answered.

"Then tell me about this mystery you were working on, the one about the sheriff and the dead man."

"You remember that?" I asked, feeling surprised that she would be so clear about our first meeting.

"Darling, my hip is injured, not my brain." She slid over a little in the bed.

"Yes, that's right," I said, wondering if I had offended her with my suggestion that she would be mentally incapacitated.

"Well, I'm more confused than I was yesterday," I said as I stretched out my legs.

"Yes, but you're different than you were yesterday."

I wasn't sure what she meant so I asked. "How so?"

"Thomas Sawyer is how so," she replied.

I blushed.

"How is it that everybody knows about me and Tom?" I asked. "It just happened last night."

"It's hard to hide that kind of splendor," she said, a big grin stretched across her face. "And I know good love when I see it."

"Well, it really isn't all that interesting now because I've probably gone and blown it all to pieces," I responded, remembering what I had stolen from this man I was supposed to love, then how I told the deputy.

"Why, child? What have you done?" she asked, sounding quite alarmed.

"I listened to you, is what I've done."

She seemed confused so I explained.

"I trusted someone, like you suggested. And I'm not sure that he's the one I should have." I crossed my legs at the ankles.

"When did I tell you that?" she asked.

"A little while ago, before I went downstairs to get something to eat."

She didn't respond.

"You said, 'You need to trust somebody, Rose Franklin,'" I repeated her earlier words.

"Well, dear, it looks as if you were right after all. There has been a brain injury. I don't remember ever saying that to you."

Then she coughed a bit, clearing her throat. "What was the context of these words of wisdom?" she asked.

I recalled the conversation to her.

She nodded, but I could tell she didn't remember. She paused a few minutes.

"Well, it's just a beginner's mistake," she finally said. "You'll get another try."

"I'm not sure, Ms. Lou Ellen. This may have been a huge mistake," I confessed.

She moved over a little in the bed. I could tell it hurt, but she reached out and took me by the hand.

"Tell me what you've done," she said, sounding like a priest hearing confession.

I took in a deep breath, hating myself for what I was about to tell.

"I went over to Tom's trailer to find some jewelry I had left—" I stopped, realizing I was implicating myself as a woman who had slept with a man.

The older woman didn't seem phased by this information, so I continued.

"When I was there, I found a gold coin, in a book he had read to me. I stole it because I thought maybe he had something to do with Mr. Franklin's death."

I knew my story needed further explanation.

"Tom told me that story about the slave's gold, about Percy Dalton and the Quaker. And then I learned that Mr. Franklin was trying to find a burial ground. I think the two stories are related and that Tom and Mr. Franklin had found them both, and then—" I stopped.

Ms. Lou Ellen was shaking her head quite dramatically.

"What?" I asked.

"What kind of gold coin did you find?" she asked.

"A twenty-dollar piece, from Colorado. From that company that Percy Dalton got his money. A gold coin from 1860," I said.

"Was Pike's Peak on one side?" she asked.

I looked at her, surprised. I nodded slowly.

"The word *Denver* stamped beneath it?" she asked.

I nodded again, sitting up in the chair and completely facing the older woman.

She laughed. "Dear, I gave Thomas that coin."

"What?" I asked.

"Five or ten years ago after he told me that story of the slave's gold." She pulled on her sheets. "I asked around to some friends of mine who collect those old coins."

"What?" I repeated.

"I bought one of those coins from a Denver coin collector for Thomas. There's about ten or fifteen of them and I got one." She rubbed her hand across the edges of the tape on the IV site on her wrist.

"Darling," she said quietly when she could see my disbelief, "I have a lot of money."

I shook my head. "Why?" I asked, not knowing what else to say.

"Married well," she answered, as if I had asked her about how she had gotten to be rich. "More than a few times," she added.

"No, why did you give a gold coin to Thomas?" I asked.

"Oh, because Thomas and I have a close connection," she said.

I could tell she was measuring what else she was going to say. "We visit quite regularly, have common issues." She sighed.

I thought for a minute.

"AA," I said, remembering his addiction, that he said that he relied greatly on the support of others.

"Are you his sponsor?" I asked.

She raised her eyebrows, brought a finger to her lip to demonstrate a need for confidentiality. Then she smiled at me.

"Thomas reached a great milestone several years ago and I decided to honor it with a token."

"You gave him the gold coin," I said, still finding all this hard to take in.

"Thomas is a fine young man," she said. "He deserves some happiness."

I felt a deep, sinking feeling.

"Oh, no," I said, realizing what I had done, realizing that the coin might be gone for good.

"What, dear?" she asked.

"I've done an awful thing," I confessed.

"Darling, we've all done those."

She patted me again on the arm. "That's why mercy takes your breath away."

I dropped my head into my hands. "He'll never forgive me," I said.

"Well, you can't know that until you ask," Ms. Lou Ellen said. Then she yawned.

"You should go to him as soon as you can. It'll all work out," she added. She rested her head against the pillow.

"I think I may go back to sleep a little bit." She slid down in the bed.

I stood up and lowered her bed to make her more comfortable. I reached over her head and turned off her light.

I sat in the darkness, thinking what I needed to do next, considering my options, going through my wrongful actions. I had made a grave error of judgment about Thomas and I feared I had made another, perhaps one more dangerous, regarding the deputy I had trusted.

I was short on ideas. I leaned back against that hospital chair, trying to figure a way out of the mess I had created, trying to think of what I should do next. I sat like that for more than an hour trying to sort through my thoughts and actions, my misdeeds.

I pulled a blanket around me, growing more and more comfortable in my position, and before I knew it, I had fallen sound asleep.

THE FOURTH DAY

O Lord, I pray Thee
Hear my humble prayer and watch over
These, Thy Children.

Shades of your image by night
Standing by these Jordan banks
Guide them with Thy perfect Light
Until we take leave of this place.

Bound now by evil's snare
Thereby in time finding our freedom
Heaven's still waters running fair
Finally, to see Thy face.

TWENTY-ONE

I slept for almost three hours and when I awoke, everything was clear. The yellow sun rising, thin pink layers of light streaming across the sky, the tiny drips in the line falling from the bag of fluids and into Ms. Lou Ellen's veins, the easy way morning creeps across a room. Everything was clear.

I remembered where I heard the last name of the ambulance attendant, Kunar, the driver who was supposedly taking the dead body to Nashville, then finally delivering it all cleaned-up to Little Rock, the white sand that was from the quarry, the Kunar Quarry, and the white sand that was at first present and now mysteriously missing from Mr. Franklin's airways. The red marking ribbon in his pocket, the kind he used to mark graves, or as he was doing on the occasion of wearing the suit that day, an old burial site.

The quick, knowing way that Deputy Fisk handled the gold coin when I gave it to him, sticking it so easily in his front

pocket, the announcement of the findings in the unreported autopsy, the cold, sly way he said my father's name. Like he knew
him, knew what would make him proud. The easy way he
placed his hand on my shoulder. Like he knew me, like he had
me. It was all clear and simple.

It was as if the sleep loosened my thoughts, unraveled my
doubts, and placed them in an ordered row in front of me. As if
an angel jumped down from a tree and walked with me a ways,
pointing things out, giving depth and meaning to everything
that happened along the path of my life.

It was like having somebody guiding me through dark,
muddy waters and finally helping me up on the banks of a river
where the darkness and the night noises and the way we never
spoke as we drifted, suddenly made perfect sense. It was like
knowing the thing you cannot say and then finally finding the
right words. It's like the outing of truth. When it finally comes,
there's no way to mistake it. Everybody who witnesses it knows
exactly what it is.

I stood up from the hospital recliner where I had enjoyed
such deep sleep and folded up the blanket I had placed around
me. The patient was still resting soundly so I did not disturb her.
I walked over and found my bag, washed my face, brushed my
teeth, and prepared myself for what I knew I was going to have
to do that morning.

I stood at the window and prayed, to the river, to the tree angel, to the saints waiting on the other side, to God. "Somebody,
please don't let it be too late."

Ms. Lou Ellen woke up when Maria came in, her last visit before her shift ended and together we got the patient up, took her for a few painful steps around the bed, and then positioned her as comfortably as we were able to in the large chair where I had been for most of the night.

"Did you sleep, dear?" she asked as I threw the blanket around her.

"I feel like a new woman," I said, thinking that there was also energy to this newfound clarity.

"How about you?" I asked the patient, hoping the same for her.

"No, I still feel like an old woman."

She winced when she shifted in her chair.

I helped change the bed linens and then I gave her a quick bath and a fresh gown. I combed her hair and because she insisted, helped her apply a little makeup. By the time Rhonda and Lucas arrived, at six A.M., she was already worn out from her morning activities, but looking forward to breakfast.

"Dear sister," Lucas said when he walked in. "Don't you look spectacular?" He leaned next to her and kissed her on top of the head.

"Hey, Mama," Rhonda said, walking in behind her husband. Then she turned to me. "How did things go last night?"

Before I could answer, Ms. Lou Ellen spoke up.

"Lucas, you take Rose back to Shady Grove," his mother-in-law instructed. "She has things she needs to do."

And she winked at me as if she had received the same clarity I had in knowing exactly what I needed to accomplish.

She already knew that I had tried Thomas on the cell phone

several times without success and was growing anxious to return to West Memphis and make sure that he was okay. And even though she didn't know all the details of what had happened, what I had done, what I had set into motion, she knew I was in a hurry to get to him

"I thought I'd pray with you first, dear sister," Lucas said as I stood at the door waiting for my ride.

"You pray with Rose while you're driving her across the bridge," she said. "She needs to see Tom."

Rhonda and Lucas both peered at me with unknowing looks, but Lucas agreed to take me back and then told his wife he would return by lunchtime. I hugged the women good-bye.

There was not too much traffic on the bridge, but I could feel myself getting more and more worried as we drove toward the state line. I was sure that I had waited too long. I said to Lucas, "Brother, I need you to pray."

"Okay," he said, seeming a bit unsure of my request. And the big man drove and prayed. He prayed for salvation and hope and mercy and grace. He prayed for Ms. Lou Ellen, for Rhonda, for the Miller family, for Thomas, and for me. Mostly he prayed for me. Eyes open, alert to his driving, he prayed like a preacher. He prayed like the righteous man that Mary said he was.

He prayed like a brother, like a friend; I knew that I had been wrong about Lucas. He was not at all how he looked, not at all as his history made him seem. And once we were off the interstate and headed in the direction of Shady Grove, I was actually hopeful about the man and his prayer. I considered the possibility that somebody had heard him.

He took the exit, drove down the paved road to the cutoff to the campground and then drove along the path to Tom's trailer, where I had asked him to take me first. When we got there, the front door was open and I knew we were seeing the fruits of trouble.

"Call the sheriff," I said as I ran inside to see if Tom was still there. I knew Lucas had a cell phone because I had seen it strapped to his belt.

The trailer had been ransacked. Books down from the shelves, drawers pulled out and emptied. Every room had been searched and turned inside out. Deputy Fisk had already gotten there, and then I was sure that Thomas was in great peril.

"Did you call the sheriff?" I asked frantically as Lucas walked up the steps to the trailer.

He stood at the door, examining the front room. "Lord Jesus," he said. "What has happened?"

"Lucas!" I yelled at him. "Did you call the sheriff?"

He stood shaking his head in disbelief.

"He's not in," he reported. "I just left a message."

Then he stammered a bit, "I didn't know this had happened."

"Call him again," I said. "Call him again and tell him there's been a murder."

"A murder?" Lucas asked. "Dear little sister, why would anybody murder Thomas?"

"Just call him!" I screamed.

He pulled out his phone and dialed a number.

I realized that he had called 911 when he said that he had an emergency to report.

"No!" I yelled. "Not nine-one-one!" I remembered what the deputy had said about one scanner, that everyone heard the incoming calls. I was worried that he could get to us first.

Lucas stopped the call and threw up his hands, like he didn't know what to do. He was shaking.

"Call his direct line," I said, trying to act calm. "Call him at home; just don't call nine-one-one."

He shook his head at me. Then I thought of something, thought of where Thomas might be.

"Do you have the key to the lock on the quarry fence?"

The big man was still staring at the mess in the trailer.

"Lord Jesus," he kept saying, sucking his teeth.

"Lucas!" I yelled, "Do you have the key?"

"Yes, sister, it's on my ring." He reached in his pocket and took out his keys. He stopped for a minute.

"No, wait, I gave it to somebody"—he stopped as if he was thinking—"I loaned it to Lawrence Franklin. I never got it back. I'll have to get the master from the office."

"Then, hurry, go get it and meet me there," I said, because now I knew Thomas would be at the quarry.

I pushed him out of the trailer and off the steps.

Lucas jumped into his truck and drove off to Shady Grove. I ran as fast as my legs could take me down the path and over to the far side of the pond.

I ran first to the chair that was hidden at the edge of the woods. Nothing had changed around there since I had first noticed it. Then I ran over to the fence that wrapped around the quarry. I could see tire tracks near the gate and I tried to wiggle my way through a couple of openings. I was too big. I ran around the fence, calling out for Tom. I heard nothing but noises from the river. I moved out in the tall weeds.

Finally, as I turned a corner, following the fence as it neared the banks of the Mississippi, still calling out Tom's name, I saw a place at the bottom that had been bent, an opening forced beneath it. It was just big enough that I was able to crawl through.

The sun was full and high in the morning sky. The temperature was already rising. I felt the sweat bead across my forehead as I pulled myself up from the ground where I had rolled under the fence and into the quarry grounds. I stood up, shook the dust from my clothes and without knowing where to go, headed on a narrow path that led between two mounds of rock.

There were three bulldozers parked near one of the hills. I walked around them and headed to the giant hole where the rock was being excavated. It was about twenty-feet wide and I couldn't see from the spot where I was standing how deep it was cut.

So I walked closer. Just as I neared the edge, something caught my eye and I glanced over my right shoulder and noticed an area that appeared to be freshly dug. There was a stake with a red ribbon, just like the ribbon in Lawrence's pocket, tied around it, marking the location.

As I moved over toward it, I saw a small stack of bones next to a mound of dirt and then a pair of feet roped together, sticking out from the other side. I hurried around the hill and there was Tom, roughed-up, tied-up, and looking very anxious.

"Oh, Lord, Thomas." I hurried to him and checked his wounds.

He had been beaten pretty badly around his eyes and nose. A large knot was on the back of his head. There was a little blood and a lot of swelling. I yanked off the tape that was wrapped around his mouth.

"Hurry," he said as the tape pulled off. "Hurry, they're on the way back by now."

I tried untying the rope around his arms, but the knot was too tight.

"Where are they gone?" I asked. And then, "I'm so sorry," I kept saying, "this is all my fault."

"Rose." His voice was raised, sharp. "Just help me up, there's a shovel and a hoe behind that hill of dirt, get it and try to cut the rope around my feet. I told them the gold was at the funeral home. They've been gone for more than an hour, they'll be back soon."

I turned to the hill.

"Hurry!" he repeated. "We don't have a lot of time." He tried to pull himself up.

But before I could get the shovel or find the hoe, before I could see a means of getting Thomas untied, someone else had already gotten to it.

I turned just in time to see a woman holding the tool above her head, aiming it right in my direction. She was straining as she brought it down.

The last thing I remember thinking was, This was the kind of morning my father loved.

Thomas called out my name and I fell into a pile of old bones.

TWENTY-TWO

I crossed the Jordan River by walking. There was no boat or skiff or captain to lead me across. I stepped in the water and the water held me up, like mountain rock and desert sand and hard dirt surfaces. I glided across. The water shimmered in the light of a perfect sun. The blue below and the blue above were one and the same, indistinguishable, only a faint silver line dividing one from the other.

I walked because I knew I was being called. And I did not hurry because I understood that I had all the time I would ever need. The other side, the one where I was heading, was green and rolling. It was the prettiest land I had ever seen and the only reason I picked up my pace as I moved across the flat blue plain of water was just to lay myself down in that carpet of rich, emerald green.

I was halfway across when people starting coming over the hills, watching as I headed in their direction. Families of people were dressed in long white robes, as if candidates for baptism waiting in line, some holding hands, others waving at me, welcoming me to the banks of their still, blue river, the edge of the land of dark rolling green.

I saw people I recognized, but could not name. Children and old women who looked familiar, who seemed to know me, and whom I seemed to know; as I neared the shore I grew more and more eager to get to them, to find out who they were and how we had gone missing from one another.

They lined the banks. So many to greet me. So many waiting for me. And as I scanned the crowd, I saw the small group gathered in front, the chosen few, the ones whom I knew without consideration. Jolie Miller. Lawrence Franklin. Grandma Freeman. Papa Burns. And her.

Long, thick hair, sturdy brown eyes, thin nose, and wide, reaching arms; she was the one I hurried for, the one I lifted my feet faster and faster for and raced toward. She was the one who had been calling me and I would not be turned away. She was the pearl of great price, the treasure in the field. I would have sold everything I own to get to her.

She had not changed since I last remembered, and when she smiled the sky opened itself in flashes of light. And I hurried. Ran, flew, jumped. And just as I reached out to her, she blew a kiss, nodded her approval at who I had become, and a ribbon of color, red as dark as blood, pulled me away. The kiss still wet upon my cheek.

I awoke to a room of eager faces.

"Praise the Lord," sounded a familiar booming voice. "Little sister has opened her eyes."

Lucas Boyd stood the closest. His bald white head reflecting the light above the bed. His wife stood beside him. The lines of worry softened across their faces.

Mary was there. Janice Miller was there. A red-faced sheriff stood near the door, and a nurse, Maria, was bent across me, pulling at the sleeve of a blood pressure cuff that was wrapped across my left arm.

My head ached. My fingers tingled. And as I tried to move from one riverbank to another, from side to side, the thoughts and the memories drifted in slow, confusing lines.

"Tom Sawyer?" I asked, the words thundering in my head, but falling from my lips apparently in just a whisper because Lucas bent very near my face to hear me say the name again.

"Tom Sawyer?"

"Oh, little sister, he's just fine," the big man answered. "He's two doors down, with a lump on his head not much smaller than yours, a few cuts on his arms, and a big wide heart waiting to know you're okay, too."

A tear fell from the corner of my eye. I couldn't explain. It was like leaving home and finding home all in the same second. Losing love and falling right back into it. It was all of life in one dive down and deep into the arms of a blue-brown river and then a jump straight up into the white sky. It was more than I could hold in the space of my mind.

"What happened?" I asked, trying not to move my head.

"Pssst." That sound was familiar.

"You almost got yourself killed." It was Mary. She was standing on the other side next to the nurse.

"Rose, dear." Ms. Lou Ellen was there somewhere in the room. I couldn't find her, but I certainly recognized her voice.

"You figured it out," she said. "You led the sheriff right to the guilty party and you are a great hero."

"What?" I asked.

"Doesn't matter," a gruff voice spoke from the door of the room. I took it to be that of the sheriff.

"We just want to make sure you're okay," he said. He actually sounded concerned.

"Mr. Kunar, the manager at the quarry, had told his family a couple of weeks ago that the undertaker was looking around, that it seemed he had uncovered some old historical site. That was when the deputy and his girlfriend started watching Mr. Lawrence because they thought he had found the gold."

Rhonda was recounting the events for me. I recalled being at the place with the marking, the place where I got hit on the head, and I knew then for sure that he had found the burial ground.

"They saw him digging at the quarry a few times earlier in that week and decided that he had finally discovered Dalton's treasure. They followed him the morning he disappeared. On his way to St. Louis, he had stopped off at the quarry just to mark the spot he had located, and then was on his way back to drop off the key with Lucas at the campground."

She waited a second to let me catch up.

"He was marking the burial ground, not the hidden gold," I said, trying to put everything together. "He used red ribbon."

"Right," Rhonda answered. "There's no reason to think he knew anything about gold." She added, "But Fisk didn't know that."

"Apparently, after he had marked his spot that morning, he went down to the river, we think maybe to wash his hands before heading out of town. When he returned to the quarry he saw the deputy and the paramedic digging where he had marked his findings. When he surprised them and asked them what they were doing, the deputy knocked him on the head, kinda like you." She smiled. "But unfortunately, he fell and landed in the quarry and drowned."

"The girl confessed," the sheriff said. "She tampered with the dead body and with the autopsy. Fisk was the main one. He just wanted to get rich. I don't think they meant to kill Mr. Franklin, but it's murder just the same."

I could see his red face fall. "Damn shame," he added.

"Anyway, you're fine now. You're okay." Lucas had reached down and taken my hand.

"What about the gold?" I asked.

"Thomas was returned his coin," Ms. Lou Ellen reported. I finally saw her sitting in a wheelchair near Mary.

"The rest of it was never lost," Lucas added.

"Tom said he tried to tell you about it yesterday afternoon before you came over to the hospital. He had heard about some old slave papers that had been found at the courthouse in Vicksburg, Mississippi, and he had somebody make copies and send them to the courthouse here.

"Turns out they were old bills of sale of slaves from there. And just like he hoped, there were three of them written for Daltons. One woman, Lavender, and her two children Percy, Jr., and Lydia. The Quaker must have made it because the Daltons got their freedom. They were reunited after all."

The room was spinning. I remembered how Thomas had something he had wanted to tell me, but I wouldn't let him. I was filled with guilt for not being truthful to him, for not trusting him, and I was glad that I would be able to apologize, that I had the chance to tell him I was sorry. Then I recalled where I had just come from, who and what I had seen.

I looked around the room for Janice. She was standing at the foot of the bed.

"I saw Jolie," I said to the young woman.

She smiled and took hold of my leg.

"She's happy," I said. "She's not alone, not at all."

The young mother nodded. "Clara sends her love," she said. "She's back at the camper, but still a little sore from the procedure."

I was glad to know that she was okay. "Lawrence Franklin," I said to those standing around me.

"He's okay, too." I squeezed Lucas's hand. "Tell Ms. Eulene, Lucas, Lawrence is okay, too."

He nodded. And I glanced around the room at those who had gathered there to be with me and I remembered how I felt

D

O

NWN

BY THE RIVERSIDE

when I stood outside Ms. Lou Ellen's door after her surgery and I realized that I now rested in my own circle of grace, that I had family, that I wasn't alone any longer. I closed my eyes to rest.

And then I fell asleep.

Deeply, peacefully. No rivers to cross, no mysteries to solve. No leaving and no arriving.

Just sleep.

ANOTHER DAY

My bones are weary, long to sleep
If only there is room to keep
These thoughts, these dreams, this flesh, this heart
A resting ground I need not depart
A place where familiar souls abide
Here, down by the riverside.

TWENTY-THREE

They say that death changes a person, but I wouldn't say that it was dying that did it to me. I'd say it was love.

I attended two funerals in the same afternoon in West Memphis, Arkansas. Both of them at the side of Thomas Sawyer, who forgave me my misjudgment of his character and for the way in which I chose not to trust him.

"Sword and shield," is what he said as he reached over and took me by the hand when I told him I was sorry.

"It's much too burdensome to try and carry around all that weight of unforgiveness." And we walked along the path out of Shady Grove and over to the Antioch Holiness Church to Lawrence Franklin's service.

I guess the deacon and the Franklin family forgave their preacher for his erroneous ways, too, because he preached like a man who recognized and received grace. He spoke about Lawrence Franklin as the heartbeat of the southside community, as the one who drew them together, not just with those living on this shore of the river, but also with those who had long crossed over.

He said that Lawrence Franklin made sure every deceased person found a resting place in West Memphis and that because his life had been so intricately tied to goodness, so completely connected to finding lost souls a home, that he was sure to have found his own path of righteousness out of the valley of the shadow of death and into the light of everlasting life.

He said that the church and the Boyds were sponsoring the Memorial Grounds out by Shady Grove where Mr. Franklin had indeed found the burial site of a boatload of slaves, that in Lawrence's honor it would be recognized by the community and the town and that it would be a place of rest for both the living and the dead.

I smiled at the thought of that, knowing that dedicating that place, laying claim to those lost lives, was the only thing the undertaker really ever wanted. I thought about him placing that piece of red ribbon in his pocket, sealing the promise he made to those who had died. And I was sure he was pleased and that somewhere on the banks of the Jordan, he was celebrating what had finally come to pass.

The church service was beautiful and fitting; and even though I received a fair number of sideway glances and stares, I accepted Ms. Eulene Franklin's offer and sat with her as family in the very front row. She said that Lawrence would have wanted it that way, that he would have welcomed me as kin and that because of her son's kind witness to how we treat family, she could do no less. I was honored and I wept as if I knew him because in an unspoken way, I did.

The entire funeral procession left the church and the Franklins' gathering and walked in a long shifting line to Shady Grove, down to the river. We walked carrying bowls of fresh peas, pots of greens, fried chicken, and pitchers of tea.

We walked like the children of Israel sent out of Egypt and down to the Red Sea. We walked in a common spirit of kinship and goodwill and we walked to where Lucas had lined up rows of chairs, the choir from the Shining Light Baptist Church, and tables to leave our food. We all took our places along with the others from the campground to move from remembering a man who brought families together and who honored life to remember a little girl who conversed with angels.

Janice and Frank Miller were a long ways from being healed of their misery, but they joined in the singing and the praying as they held on tightly to their youngest daughter, Clara, who was so assured of her sister's wholeness that she relied on it for her family's repair. They stood surrounded by folks they didn't know, but folks they knew cared for them, for their loss, and for their broken hearts.

After the river service, Jolie's funeral, we stood around and ate plates of shared food. We walked down to the quarry where the fence was brought down and out to the place where the old bones of slaves and ancestors had been buried once again. Then we returned to the tents and I met people from the south side of West Memphis and folks who claimed they owed their lives to the Boyds and the second chances they had received at Shady Grove.

Mary acted as the official host, hurrying from task to task, filling glasses with ice and rearranging trays and dishes. Rhonda and Lucas sat with the Millers, and even welcomed the sheriff and his brother, who had come over to make their peace and offer their condolences to those who were bereaved.

Ms. Lou Ellen sat near the dessert table with Mrs. Franklin and as I glanced around at the strangers becoming friends, she waved her little finger at me. I stood leaning against the tree and I smiled and waved back.

Tom walked over, bringing two folding chairs, and we sat down and watched without words as the river rolled past. It wasn't very long before Clara ran over and fell into my lap.

"We're leaving tomorrow," she said, throwing her arms around my neck. "I've got school soon, and Mama and Daddy have to go back to work."

"Yes, I know," I answered, sliding my chin across the top of her head.

"Where you going?" she asked, having noticed that my Bronco was fixed and was parked beside my camper.

I saw Tom look in my direction.

"I don't think I'm going anywhere right away," I said.

The little girl lifted her head up and faced me. Her brown eyes studied me.

"Is it because of him?" she asked, pointing at Tom.

I laughed.

"Well, yes," I answered. "And because I said I would stay and look after Ms. Lou Ellen while Mary goes to visit her family for a couple of weeks."

By then I had learned that Lucas and Rhonda were gone from Shady Grove so much because they stay on the river visiting a lot of the ex-convicts who live up and down the Mississippi.

They check on them regularly, counsel them, bring them groceries, loan them money. They consider their river work to be their ministry and I respect the kindness they spread.

I thought about the little girl's question and I added, "I'm also staying because I like it here."

Clara remained in that position for a few minutes, watching the people at the tents, watching me and Tom, and then stood up, turned around and sat again in my lap, this time facing the same direction I was, out toward the river.

"It's a good place to be, Rose," she said, sounding so much older than her years.

"Yeah?" I said. "What makes you think so?" I asked.

"Well, with all these people coming and going at a camp-ground and I guess especially the ones who stay a long time"— she turned and looked again at Tom, then she leaned her head against my shoulder—"you'll never be alone."

I squeezed my arms around her waist and watched the river run past.

And I knew she was right.

There's a community here. Rhonda, Lucas, Mary, Ms. Lou Ellen, Tom, some of the others I've met around the camp-ground, Leonard Elton and Old Man Willie, the ones who fish or hang out at the water, they're all connected somehow.

They got something holding them together. Deep. Long lasting. A bond that ties lost souls together and anchors them hard and strong to somebody, to something that will not let them go.

I know most of the folks from my hometown would look down their noses at all of us making our home at Shady Grove. They'd call us river rats or trailer trash or homeless folks living on the fringe of society, but I don't care. I love this place and the people here. It's the most genuine hospitality I've ever experienced.

It's true, I thought, as I sat with the little girl watching the muddy river. I might not understand where I came from or where I was heading, but I certainly knew where I was.

I am Rose Franklin and I'm in West Memphis, Arkansas, at the Shady Grove Campground. I am sitting right on the banks of the Mississippi River, surrounded by the ones I now call my family.

I'm wrapped up tight in the arms of love.

Read more about Rose
and the folks at Shady Grove
in Jackie Lynn's next book

❦

Turn the page
for a sneak preview of
JACOB'S LADDER,
coming June 2007 from
St. Martin's Press.

ONE

It was late when the old Ford pickup pulling a small travel trailer drove up to the office at Shady Grove, the campground situated on the Mississippi River in West Memphis, Arkansas. Mary always locked the door at 8:00 P.M., and any campers arriving after hours had to make their own arrangements regarding where to park. They were asked to put one night's payment in an envelope kept in a bucket by the front window, stuff the envelope through a slot in the door, and select a site from the large map pinned next to the after-hours directions.

Rose was usually the one to follow up by stopping at the site the next morning to find out how long the campers were planning to stay and whether or not they were satisfied with their hookups. Being late March, still well before the busy summer season, there were usually plenty of places from which to choose.

Jacob Sunspeaker was the driver of the old truck, a 1974

model, blue and white, with New Mexico tags. He came from the southern tip of McKinley County, west of El Morro and just beyond Ramah. He was of the Zuni tribe, lived in the pueblo, in a small house beside his sister and her family. He made jewelry—bracelets and rings mostly, some belt buckles, all silver with an inlay design—which he sold in Gallup. That was where he bought his truck and trailer in the early nineties, when he was particularly productive and when the silver business was booming.

The trailer he was pulling, a Coachmen, was rusted on the bottom and its gray paint was peeling on the front and sides. It was a twenty-four-footer, with a double bed, a table, and extra storage—plenty of room for two people, more than was really needed for just one.

He took it to the market where he sold his bracelets and rings and over to Santa Fe and Albuquerque for the Indian Market and to some of the feast days at the pueblos, where he participated in the dances and got new ideas for his jewelry designs. He lived in it most of the summers, moving to his house only when the wind blew too hard, making it difficult to sleep or cook in a house on wheels.

The Coachmen suited Mr. Sunspeaker. Once he had received the vision that became his mission and when the knowledge of what he had to do became the sturdy place from which to hoist himself, he found the travel trailer was the best possible means of always being ready to relocate and visit the next necessary destination. He discovered that he liked the feel of being mobile, of having a dwelling that moved so effortlessly with him.

His sister teased him about taking up the habits of white people, so many of whom they saw driving their campers and trailers through the pueblo to get to the Hawikuh Ruins or Ojo Caliente, the hot springs near their homes. But her jokes never bothered him.

He told her that the ease of few belongings and the ability to move quickly was more the way of Indians, he having descended from a people who traveled as nature dictated.

The old Coachmen was dented in a few places, in need of a good wash, and two of the windows were cracked and covered with silver duct tape. Jacob Sunspeaker, however, was satisfied with both how it looked and how it pulled behind his old truck. He saw no need for an upgrade or a fresh coat of paint.

No one knew exactly what time he drove into the campground. Old Man Willie, who lived in one of Rhonda and Lucas's campers situated near the office, was usually the one who confirmed the times of arrival. Generally awake until very late, he stopped by the office every day and informed the manager on duty what time the after-hours visitors arrived.

That night, however, the raw, moonless night that Jacob Sunspeaker found his way from the interstate over to the river, Willie didn't hear the truck and the travel trailer pull in and stop. He was in bed, having eaten a very big dinner, and had been lulled to sleep by the extended winter chill and the black night of the March sky.

He was dreaming of violets and an old lover's smooth hands when the Coachmen pulled over to site number Thirty-four, one without hookups on the far right side of the campground, the grassy area near the Mississippi and close to the uncleared part of the acreage.

Originally used for tents and people sleeping in their automobiles, that part of the campground had been closed for more than a year. The narrow piece of real estate owned by the Boyd couple jutted out farther into the Mississippi at that location and had been added to their purchase without their request. Over the years, the property had developed so many flooding problems that instead of trying to remedy them, Rhonda and Lucas had simply discontinued using that landing for camping sites.

Only hikers and the guests who enjoyed private fishing visited the spot, but there was still a driveway leading to it. Apparently, Mr. Sunspeaker had not paid attention to the map at the office and had driven down on the main road, past the curve that led into the park, and turned right onto the old driveway and into the closed-off area.

Willie had awakened because of a barking dog and was sad to be yanked away from a woman's arms and the dream he loved so much. Because he was awake, he did hear the other vehicle that pulled in just after Mr. Sunspeaker.

He peeked out the window just in time to see the one with the idling motor, the black SUV with unidentified license plates. He paid no attention to it, assuming it was an automobile belonging to a registered guest or that it was just someone visiting a friend. He knew cars came and went at Shady Grove as the campers enjoyed nightly excursions to Memphis and other places along the river.

Since he was not familiar with Mr. Sunspeaker and his journey to Arkansas, Willie had no way of knowing that the SUV was the same vehicle that had been parked on the pueblo for a week as the old man prepared for his journey, the same vehicle that had followed Jacob Sunspeaker out of New Mexico.

He also did not know the old man had seen the trouble coming to him in a dream in the form of a dark thundercloud and that Mr. Sunspeaker had pushed up his trip by more than a couple of days, trying to elude what he saw on the horizon.

Willie simply got back into bed, rolled over, and went back to sleep before noticing that the driver turned off his lights as the car headed down the main road behind the old truck and trailer and that there were at least three men inside, all dressed in black, two of them carrying guns. He pulled the covers tightly around his shoulders, wondering if the dream would come to him once more, hoping his lover had not drifted too far from his memories.

No one, not even Willie, knew that trouble, like a late winter storm, had passed through the gates of Shady Grove on the chilly night in March when the sky was pitch-black, the stars and the moon hidden behind clouds.

No one other than Willie heard the SUV as it entered the campground, and no one heard it leave within one hour's time. No one witnessed the old man struggle and finally fall. No one recognized the words that passed between his lips or the anguished way he prayed.

No one saw a thing.